ZOMBIE DEFENCE

Chronicles of the Infected

RICK WOOD

Blood Splatter Press

About the Author

Rick Wood is a British writer born in Cheltenham.

His love for writing came at an early age, as did his battle with mental health. After defeating his demons, he grew up and became a stand-up comedian, then a drama and English teacher.

He now lives in Loughborough with his fiancée, where he divides his time between watching horror, reading horror, and writing horror.

Also By Rick Wood

The Sensitives

The Sensitives

My Exorcism Killed Me

Close to Death

Demon's Daughter

Questions for the Devil

Repent

The Resurgence

Until the End

The Rogue Exorcist

The Haunting of Evie Meyers

The Torment of Billy Tate

The Corruption of Carly Michaels

Blood Splatter Books

Psycho B*tches

Shutter House

This Book is Full of Bodies

Home Invasion

Haunted House

Woman Scorned

This Book is Full of More Bodies

The Devil's Debt

Perverted Little Freak

Cia Rose

When the World Has Ended

When the End Has Begun

When the Living Have Lost

When the Dead Have Decayed

The Edward King Series

I Have the Sight

Descendant of Hell

An Exorcist Possessed

Blood of Hope

The World Ends Tonight

Anthologies

Twelve Days of Christmas Horror

Twelve Days of Christmas Horror Volume 2

Twelve Days of Christmas Horror Volume 3

Roses Are Red So Is Your Blood

Standalones

When Liberty Dies

The Death Club

Chronicles of the Infected

Zombie Attack

Zombie Defence

Zombie World

Non-Fiction

How to Write an Awesome Novel

Horror, Demons and Philosophy

Cover design by bloodsplatterpress.com

Copy-edited by LeeAnn @ FirstEditing.com

With thanks to my Street Team.

This book is dedicated to all those we lose in the imminent zombie apocalypse.

We'll remember you always.

BEFORE

Chapter One

Nagging, moaning, and whining. That was all this woman ever did. Even if one thing off her never-ending list of demands was completed, there would be no praise, no acknowledgement, no let-up; just a continuation of demands that seemed to have no foreseeable end.

Eugene was sick of it. Sick of everything. Sick of her, and her incessant chattering and moaning. Sick of waiting for his plan to come to fruition. Sick of knowing everything was going to change and he was going to rule the country and there was nothing he could do but wait.

This woman used to be a goddess. Seriously, at the beginning she was a slender, petite beauty who'd rub Eugene's shoulders and encourage him to pursue his ambitions. She had been soft, whilst retaining the prowess of a powerful, strong woman.

Now look at her, he thought.

Her hair had curled upwards in a way that displayed the puffiness of her overgrown cheeks. Her walk was no longer a sexy strut but a struggling waddle that took up most of the pavement. Even her ankle fat had fat. He'd watch her at night, getting undressed, remembering the way he once used to marvel at the sumptuous curves of her bare body. Now, the sight of her stretched, saggy skin bulging over the elastic waistband of her underwear made him gag. And her repulsive personality... oh boy; her personality had deteriorated even quicker than her body. Her demeanour had a similar stench to her uncared-for pits. She was abrasive, demanding, and rude.

"And after that, you need to phone the water company and get that bill changed, it's ridiculous," she continued, Eugene only focussing on the moustache hair that wobbled with each smack of her chubby lips. Her excess saliva kept coming out in bubbles, and he was terrified that one of those bubbles was going to land on his face.

"Are you even listening to me?" she demanded.

"No," Eugene replied honestly. "No, Sheila, I'm not. I don't ever listen to you. Not really."

"Well, how is that going to help our marriage? I thought Doctor Holeson told you that we have to listen and attend to each other's needs" – this went on, and on, and on, but he tuned it out and thought about other things; just as Eugene had spent numerous years learning to.

That was when he got the text.

He pulled his phone halfway out of his pocket and took a peek. He wasn't sure why he was being discreet about checking his phone; surely, she'd realise he wasn't listening. But, alas, once he'd read the message, he lifted his head to find that she was still going, yattering on about responsibilities and dependence and this and that and whatever and yadda yadda yadda.

It's done.

It was just a simple, two-word message from General Boris Hayes, but it changed everything.

The world was never going to be the same again.

He stood. Put his suit jacket on. Looked around for his keys.

"Where on earth do you think you're going?" she demanded, highly offended that he had the impudence to dare interrupt her rant. "We are still talking! We have not finished! You said we'd work on this!"

Eugene didn't even glance at her as he left the dining table where she sat and meandered toward the kitchen. She followed him.

"Honestly, what is wrong with you? I have done everything you need, and you won't even listen to me. Does it even matter to you what I'm saying? Well? Does it?"

Yadda yadda yadda.

He took the disgustingly beige apron from the back of the door and placed it carefully over his neck. He tied it in place.

"What are you doing?" she persisted. "Are you cooking?"

"No," he replied. "I am not cooking."

"Then what the hell is the apron for?"

He took a large knife out of the kitchen drawer.

"I don't want to get blood on my suit."

"What?"

"It's a nice suit."

She didn't move. He thought she'd at least run, but she didn't. She stared at the knife, then his eyes, to the knife, to his eyes.

"Eugene, what are you doing?" she asked, her stubborn rant ending and weakness overtaking her.

"What am I doing?" Eugene repeated, stepping toward her.

"Don't you love me?"

He laughed. He couldn't help it. It was a ridiculous question, and it deserved a raucous guffaw. He lifted his head back and sprayed the laughs out of his wide-open mouth. He wanted to savour this, to enjoy it, but he knew he had things to do. Best get to it.

"Eugene, I–"

She never finished her sentence.

He swung the knife straight through her cheek. It stuck there like it was stuck in thick mud and he struggled to pull it back out. Instead, he watched her, astonished. He hadn't known what to expect. Of course, he knew what he intended when he lunged the knife toward her; he intended to stab her. But, having never used a knife for such use, he wasn't sure how it was going to go. Since it was an ordinary kitchen knife, he wasn't even sure if it would do the trick – but boy, did it. The knife was visible in her open mouth, its shiny silver lodged between her teeth.

She screamed, although it was a muffled scream – she had a knife through her gob, after all.

With a large yank, Eugene withdrew the knife. It took more force to get it out than it took to put it in, which surprised him, but he wasn't sure why.

She tried say his name again, but it only made him laugh. Why was she being so silly? Her cheek had a gaping hole and her tongue was surrounded by blood. It was dripping down her chin, for God's sake! How did she expect to be able to talk?

He shook his head. *Silly bitch.*

He swung the knife again, and this time it landed in her neck. He hadn't particularly aimed it, he just hoped he'd swing it with such a circumference and such force that it would go in, and it did.

She fell to her knees.

She grabbed at the knife, trying to remove it.

Eugene couldn't be bothered to use the strength required to remove the knife, so he searched the kitchen drawers for another. Luckily, there was another, and with a blade just as sharp, too, if not more so. What a day this was!

He mounted her, placing his knees by her hips.

Her eyes peered up at him, so wide, so scared. Like a deer caught in the headlights, as the tired cliché goes. Such a cliché may be old, but there is a reason it's used so much – because it is so accurate. That is exactly what she looked like. A terrified, dumbstruck, fucking stupid deer in the headlights.

He stabbed her in the breast. Laughed as her yelp was muffled by blood. He stabbed her in the gut. In the heart. In the crotch. Everywhere he could – he just wanted to see what happened with each thrust. This was the first time he'd ever killed anyone, and as with all first times, there were, of course, learning points. He would have to do it better the next time, so he figured he may as well practise a few different places while he could, and see how well the knife landed.

That's when he heard a rustle.

He instinctively turned his head and locked onto a pair of familiar eyes peeping through the doorway.

He smiled.

His second kill had arrived.

Chapter Two

Lucy Sanders brushed her long, blond hair out of her face, smoothed down her suit, straightened her blouse, repositioned her skirt. She was about to deliver the most devastating and life-changing news she would probably ever have to deliver – now was not a time to appear tardy or unprofessional.

As the doorman opened the door, she entered the foyer and marvelled at the vast emptiness of the open room. What a huge difference there was in the way politicians lived. Yes, she worked for the government – but even so, her wage was pathetic compared to those in charge. The ceiling was high, the walls clean, and the floor a perfect marble – it was the kind of floor that made trainers squeak and heels echo. Everyone around her was either wearing a suit or dressed in perfect 'country club' gear; polo shirts, trousers ironed by their assistant, and hair swept and groomed without a strand out of place.

Most of them would be dead soon.

None of them seemed at all aware of what was happening. Then again, she wouldn't have been aware unless she had been given this message to deliver; though she was certain she'd still have noticed the heavy army presence around London. The announcement was going to be on the news in – she checked her watch – three minutes.

That's when panic would ensue.

That's why they needed their new leader in place as soon as possible. The prime minister had fallen, as had the rest of the ministers debating in Parliament with him.

How lucky for Eugene that this happened to be his day off.

She stepped into the lift, punched in the number for Eugene's floor. Luckily, it was quite high up – this gave her time to consider her words carefully.

"Eugene, there's been an outbreak," she tried.

No.

"Mr Squire, there's been–"

Should she really refer to him as mister?

"Prime Minister Squire, there has–"

But he didn't know he was prime minister yet.

Or did he? How much was he aware of? Surely he'd heard something? He must have had a text or call from someone he knew.

By the time they were done, the bustling lobby would be empty. Flats would have been evacuated with urgent haste, and people would be travelling to safety. Eugene's armed escort would have arrived and created a perimeter where those – things – couldn't get in.

What were those things, anyway?

She'd seen zombie movies. But the idea always seemed so ridiculous. Something that belonged in a comedy more than a horror.

Honestly, if she woke up and found this was all a dream, she wouldn't be–

"Shit."

She'd been too lost in thought.

She was almost there.

Right. Time to think. Prepare the words. Get ready.

Stop being the shy little girl who never spoke at school.

Stop being the pathetic little runt who got dumped by guys who would always say, "It's not you, it's me."

Stop being the person she was, basically. Have some gumption for a change. Some courage, which so seldom came to her. Be the person whose voice didn't break as they spoke, out of fear that they might just upset someone.

She tried her introduction again.

"Mr Squire, I need you to come with me. There has been–"

What?

What had there been?

The lift dinged, and the doors opened.

She paused. Waited. Took in a deep breath.

But she knew she shouldn't hang around. They had very limited time.

She stepped onto the floor. Felt the soft carpet press against her toes. Was this the best time to wear heels? Were they going to have to run?

She scoffed. Was this really what she was thinking about right now? Her footwear?

She passed a few rooms where the doors were open. Families were frantically packing suitcases. Parents were kneeling beside their children, telling them they needed to be calm. Behind them, the television was playing.

The report had aired. Everyone knew.

It suddenly felt very real.

She could have denied it to herself before, maybe – but not any longer. The news was out, and life would never be the same. The country was under the control of the army, who were recommending that all civilians barricade their homes. Do not try to get to loved ones, do not try to leave your home, do not let anyone in – everyone for themselves.

She reached Eugene's door. Inhaled. Balled her fist and pronounced a few clear knocks.

There was no response.

Was he okay?

She tried again.

Nothing.

What if he'd been caught? He was the next living person in line to become prime minister; they needed leadership. Surely, he'd be all right?

She knocked once more.

Nothing.

She placed her hand upon the door handle and pressed down gently. The door was open, allowing her to slide it gently ajar. She peered in.

From where she was, she could see the kitchen.

She heard something. A commotion.

Were the infected already in here? Were they being attacked?

She readied herself to shut the door and run, she just needed visual confirmation first, she just needed to be sure; they needed a leader, and if their leader was dead, then they needed to know.

She leant in further, ever so slightly.

That's when she saw it.

A pool of blood seeping into the cracks between the kitchen tiles. At the end of this pool of blood was Sheila Squire, Eugene's wife.

Above her was Eugene. Going mad. Hysterical. With a knife. Stabbing. His wife. Stabbing his wife.

She gasped.

Eugene lifted his head and looked at her. Locked her eyes with his.

She turned and ran, only to find herself slam into the large, muscular torso of General Boris Hayes.

"General!" she yelped frantically, so pleased that he was there. "You have to help!"

He raised his eyebrows and pointed his ear toward her, as if to show he was ready to listen.

"Eugene Squire, he – he –"

He raised his eyebrows further, showing that he was waiting.

"He killed his wife!"

Hayes didn't react. At first. Then he grinned.

She was confused.

Instinct took over.

She turned to run, but Hayes effortlessly took hold of her arm and kept her in place.

Eugene appeared at the door. He wore an apron covered in blood. He took it off, revealing his fresh, clean suit, with a few droplets of red left on his face.

"Eugene," Hayes said. "We have our test subject."

Eugene clapped his hands together and cheered.

"Wonderful!" he said. "This way!"

He closed the door to his flat and led the way, followed by Hayes dragging Lucy helplessly behind him.

Chapter Three

Since they knew Lucy was going to die anyway, they evidently didn't care what she heard – and since she was locked in the boot of the car, she assumed they believed she heard very little of it. Eugene and Hayes still attempted to encrypt most of what they were saying with vague chatter, but every so often a word or phrase would add a little clarity, and each dose of clarity would send a huge tremor of fear through her body.

"...when we released the infection..."

"...we didn't create what we intended..."

"...there must be a way to still use it..."

For the first part of the journey, she had pounded that metal casing with all the energy she had. Chunks of mascara clouded her vision as her tears destroyed her makeup. It all mattered so little now. Eyeshadow, lipstick, all of it – what did it matter what she looked like when she was going to die under such horrific circumstances?

And that was one thing she was certain of, yet that she could not accept: that she was going to die.

"Let me out! Let me out!" she screamed. She went to say,

"Or I'll..." then realised that she had no end to that sentence. What could she threaten them with? What leverage could she possibly hold? How could she stand up to the acting prime minister and his well-built general?

She had nothing. Nothing but the battering of the bumpy roads smacking her face against her metal imprisonment. She felt blood dripping from her nose. Like it mattered. A nose-bleed was nothing.

What must have been a sharp turn sent her flying against the other side of the car boot. She felt the metallic box closing in on her, giving her less space, restricting her. She knew it was the same size as when she had been thrown in, but it felt smaller the longer she was in it.

Sheila.

Oh, God, Sheila.

The image flashed inside her mind with a vague recollection at first, then it imprinted itself like a cinema screen stuck on a reel. It did not go away.

Sheila had been her friend. She'd held her hand through their complications. Eugene had a habit of burying himself in his work to cope with the deterioration of their marriage, and Lucy had ended up being the next best thing Sheila had to a friend. Lucy had always covered her hopeless demeanour and introverted nature with an image of professionalism and false strength that often meant distraught women would look to her for guidance; but, in that moment, thrashing helplessly against the confines of the boot, she understood how far from reality the image she projected was.

She didn't care.

She just wanted to live.

The bumps stopped. The engine died. The faint sound of two car doors gently slamming rocked the car and she waited. Waited for what, she didn't know. Fate. Surprise. Death. Whatever it was, she didn't want to confront it. She'd rather stay in the boot. At least she knew they couldn't do anything to her while the car was driving. Now their muffled voices were coming closer, and the key was in the lock, turning the lock, and it opened, the sun behind their shoulders making her squint.

They didn't even break stride in their conversation as Hayes dragged her out of the boot by her collar, as if he was emptying shopping.

"But have we got any samples yet?" asked Eugene.

"Samples?"

"Yeah, like, anyone whose genes would splice properly."

Lucy tried to kick her legs up so she could walk on them, but she was being dragged at such a pace that, no matter how much she tried, she could not find her standing. Hayes was dragging her as if it was nothing. As if it was a large sack of potatoes that wriggled in a way that was only a mild inconvenience.

"That's the kind of thing you need to ask the labbies."

"I don't want some convoluted diatribe from a scientist, Boris, I want to know what your take on their progress was."

She needed to get out of his grasp. She needed to find a way. This was her only way to escape.

She could see the fences they were going toward. They formed a perimeter. Around a building she didn't recognise, something official, something that didn't look like people escaped from.

"My take? Those things were killing everything, that's my take."

"But were there any that were better than the others?"

Finally, her feet planted on the floor, and she used them to try to run. As soon as she thought she had successfully found her balance, Hayes kicked her feet from under her and sent them flying above her head. Her spine pounded onto the harsh bumps of the cement with a discomforting *oomph*.

"This one's a wriggler," Hayes declared, smirking as he grabbed her by the neck and lifted her up. Her legs dangled beneath her, kicking out, her eyes level with his. "She's a keeper."

"Please..." she begged. "Please don't hurt me..."

Eugene laughed heartily. The kind of laughter that comes after a hilarious prank, or a witty t-shirt on a stag do.

Hayes didn't look as amused.

"Gosh," Eugene said. "I always wanted to fuck this one. I really did. Shame, really."

"We got shit to get to."

"Righty-o, let's get to it then."

Hayes hoisted her over his shoulder, carrying her effortlessly despite her continual belligerence. She bashed against his back and it seemed to do nothing. Kicked, and it didn't even unbalance him. Shouted verbal abuse, and he just spoke over it.

"So we've got London?" Eugene continued, swiping a card on the outside of the fence that allowed them inside. Two soldiers let them in and shut the gate behind them.

"Help!" Lucy beseeched the soldiers, but they did nothing.

"We have London. It's pandemonium out there."

"Excellent. Now we hit everywhere else."

"The rest of the UK?"

"Think bigger, Boris. Think bigger."

They walked toward the large building, professional, under armed guard, soldiers patrolling the perimeter. They did not enter, however. Instead, they walked the circumference of the building until they reached a large pit.

Hayes threw Lucy into it.

As soon as she landed, she leapt back up to her feet. The landing had injured something, something in the base of her back, but she ignored the pain. She had to find a way out.

And boy, did she try to find a way out.

She jumped against the walls, scraped her fingernails along

the surface, but no matter how much of a runup she got, or leap she managed, it did nothing. She was stuck in there.

She paused and looked up at them. Waiting to see what they would do next. Waiting to see how they planned for her to die.

"Right you are then," Eugene said. "We don't have all day. Time to show me how this thing works."

Hayes turned and whistled at someone behind him. Someone Lucy couldn't see.

Hayes turned back around and winked at her.

Growling. Distant growling, of something inhuman, something animalistic, but not quite. Like the low hum of a lawn mower mixed with the screeching of a cat in pain. Something obscure, out of place. Something that didn't belong.

Then it got louder. It was more than just growling, it was yapping, grumbling, snarling, snapping, weeping.

She saw it. A soldier held a metal rod with the creature fastened to the end of it via a rope around its neck. It was a person, but not. It had a head, a body, arms, and legs, like a human, but its face had nothing of humanity about it. Its skin was torn, grey, falling off the bones. It limped, falling to one side. A long, bloody slit was painted across its belly.

It wore a soldier's uniform.

"In you go," Eugene sang.

They released it, then kicked it into the pit with Lucy.

Chapter Four

Astonished. Proud. Delighted.

Pick any superlative and it would be likely to match Eugene's emotions.

As he watched the infected individual snap and bite and grasp for that irritating little woman, he couldn't help but marvel at the job they'd done.

"We can't stay here for long," Hayes said.

"I know," Eugene confirmed.

"We can use this as our place of operations, keep it concealed – but if you're acting prime minister, you've got to do it in a way that doesn't bring attention to here."

"I know."

"After all, this is the place where we plan to–"

"For Christ's sake, Boris, I said I heard you, I agree."

Eugene was too interested in watching their creation in the pit below. The cowardly woman was running to every corner of the pit, clambering to be out of the creature's clutches. Pathetic, really. It was a pit the size of a large grave, and yet she was trying to run away.

Don't people do stupid things when their life is about

to end?

Instinct is a strange compulsion. At times, it protects you. At other times, it makes you look like an utter moron.

"We should probably get you a weapon, you know," Hayes pointed out. "To keep on you. Just in case."

"This one," Eugene said to the soldier behind him, pointing at the infected. "What happened there?"

"He was a soldier. He fought off a bunch of them and they got him. I don't think he realised what they could do."

"Silly fool."

A distant rumble grew closer. Growls from the perimeter. The stench growing ever more prominent.

They were here.

"Eugene, it's my job to protect you. We need to get you a weapon, and get you away from the fence."

"I thought it was reinforced?"

"It is, and it will stand, but it's still not wise to be near it, you at least need a gun or–"

"Fine, fine!"

"The armoury is inside."

"No, no, in a moment! I want to watch this girl die first."

Eugene remained glued to the fight occurring below. The infected was now on top of the girl, out-muscling her, its jaw hanging to its face by a thin string of skin, its saliva drooping in heavy gunks onto her forehead.

The rattle of the fence caught Eugene's attention. He did a double take as he observed it, astonished.

"By God!" he exclaimed, "there are hundreds of them."

"Eugene, really, we need to get you inside."

"Yes, yes, soon."

Hayes looked around, trying to be resourceful, making sure Eugene was protected. He had an idea.

"The soldier in the pit," Hayes said, turning to the soldier behind him. "Give his gun to the prime minister."

"His gun, sir?" the soldier asked.

Hayes' anger boiled to the brim. How stupid could people be?

"Yes, his gun. Give it to Mr Squire."

"The gun?"

"Yes, the gun that the soldier, now the infected, had. Give it to the prime minister. Now."

"I..."

"You took his gun, did you not?"

"No, I didn't think–"

A gunshot echoed.

The infected dropped to the floor, revealing the woman holding the dead soldier's gun in her quivering hands. She took aim as Hayes took Eugene to the floor. A bullet sliced through the earlobe of the useless soldier standing cluelessly behind them.

By the time Hayes had drawn his weapon and crawled to the edge of the pit, it was too late. The woman had already used the body of the infected as a stepping stone. She was dangling on the edge of the pit, her arms dragging her upwards, reaching, almost there.

As soon as Hayes' face appeared, she aimed the gun and shot, forcing Hayes to duck out of the way.

"Are you okay?" he asked Eugene.

"What the heck is happening?" came the response.

The woman lifted herself up and hoisted herself over the edge.

Hayes fired.

Nothing came out.

"Bloody typical..."

He recharged his ammo. Stood. Aimed. But, by the time he'd done that, the woman was already standing in front of him with her gun aimed at his head.

And there they stood.

A Mexican standoff.

Hayes with his gun aimed at her, her with her gun aimed at him.

Waiting.

For someone to kill. Someone to die. Someone to make a move, any move.

"Let her go," Eugene instructed, still on the ground.

"What?" Hayes demanded.

"Look at the perimeter, this place is surrounded. She won't get far. If we don't kill her, they will."

Hayes nodded. It made sense. He just hated to see a target escape.

"But, sir, the information she knows, the things she's heard us say–"

"I won't tell anyone," the woman lied. "Please, I just want to get out of here."

"For Christ's sake," Eugene continued, "she won't make it past the fence. Just be done with her."

Hayes hesitated.

This sucked. But he had his instructions.

"Fine."

She backed away, both of them keeping their guns aimed, keeping their targets in sight.

As soon as she reached the corner of the building, she turned and ran.

Eugene stood. "See to it that all other government personnel are killed in the outbreak. We can't have any more loose ends. There can be no one she's able to talk to that would listen."

"Roger, sir," Hayes confirmed, watching the woman grow smaller in the distance, toward the mass of infected surrounding the compound.

Toward an imminent, undoubted, certain death.

Chapter Five

She had no idea where she was going. What she was doing. Why she was there.

She knew what she'd heard. What they'd said. Although it was hard to decipher their vague comments whilst fearing for her life, she'd acquired a general understanding that she was sure only touched the surface – but what little she knew was still enough to terrify her.

Was it really them?

Had they caused the outbreak?

And would anyone believe her if she told them?

Doesn't matter.

Not important right now.

The foreseeable future was about survival. That was it. Living, that was all that mattered.

She reached the fence. It was leaning toward her, bustling under the pressure of so many of those... things. She'd faced one of them, one that had terrified her, almost taken her life – now here were hundreds. Their hands reaching out, as if they could smell her blood, smell her fear.

What were they going to do with her should they get her?

A bullet whipped pass her shoulder and into the head of one of them, a few metres across the fence. Then another bullet. And another. And another.

She looked above herself, to the building. Snipers. Taking them out. Of course, it made sense – if this was their concealed location, their place of secret operations, they would want some of the infected to remain at the fences to keep people away; but not enough to break them down.

It would only be a matter of time until the snipers were told to target her.

She ducked to the floor, as if that would do anything. She ran to the shelter of a vehicle, yards away, an army jeep left discarded.

She focussed on her breathing.

Her adrenaline, she could not control. Her fear, she could. She had to remember that. She had to master it if she was going to survive. Push herself in a way she'd never been pushed.

She closed her eyes.

Focus on the breathing. That comes first. Need to breathe, or it's no use. No breath, no life.

Easier said than done. She was hyperventilating, wheezing against her lungs. But they were *her* lungs, and *she* needed to control them.

In. Out. In Out.

That's it.

Big, deep intake, long breath out.

She put her hands against her chest, felt her lungs inflate, deflate, her breath sucked in, then released.

That was it.

Her breathing was done.

She opened her eyes. Not just a gradual lift of her eyelids – she whipped them up like a bullet. That opening of her eyes sparked a sudden change; it was the match that lit the fire, the curling of the fist that struck the face, the roar of the war cry.

She changed. In that moment, her whole personality, her life, her abilities, transformed in the speed of her racing heart.

This suit she wore did not define her. It wasn't even close. It mattered not.

She removed the blazer. Discarded it.

What was that beneath it?

A nice, flowery blouse with a frilly pattern over the buttons?

Fuck the frilly pattern.

She straightened the sleeve. Ripped it. Tore it right up to her shoulder, where she pulled the entire sleeve right off. Then she repeated this with the other.

She undid the bottom few buttons. Ripped the circumference around the base of her breasts, throwing the useless material to the side, revealing her untouched navel. Minutes ago, she would never have had the shrewdness to reveal such a thing in public; she was too insecure about it. It bore stretch marks from a brief period of being overweight as a child, and it bore the scar of a belly ring she'd had during a vaguely rebellious adolescence, it even bore a few rolls when she crouched down – fuck those marks, fuck that scar, fuck those rolls – but, most of all, fuck that girl who sought the shadow of her peers to hide the timid wretch in the dark.

That person died in that pit.

She stood.

Ripped off those skin-coloured tights.

Ripped a slit in the side of her skirt. Exposed the outside of her thigh. She needed to run. A pencil skirt was useless to her.

And, if she needed run, she was not going to do it with heels.

She took them off. Looked them over.

Those heels were quite sharp.

She held a heel in either hand.

She looked to the infected clambering for her.

She climbed the vehicle. Prepared her jump over the fence.

Held her arms out, forming a crucifix with her body, clutching the weapons in her hand that had so far only given her cramp in her feet.

She screamed. Leapt. Landed amongst them.

They reached their arms out for her. Fought against one another to reach her, to grab her, eat her, taste her, find her.

She stuck the first heel into the throat of the closest infected.

She unseamed the next from its belly to its throat, its guts falling down her legs, sliming, dripping, painting her red.

Minutes ago, she would have gagged. Not anymore. Blood suited her. It was her colour.

She stood.

They surrounded her.

It was time to fight.

And, honestly, she kind of liked it.

AFTER

Chapter Six

There was no light. No natural light, anyway. Just the harsh sting of artificial luminosity, the fluorescent fake white of the dim bulb above.

Gus couldn't remember how long he'd been staring at it.

He was sure it was weeks. It felt like years, but it couldn't have been. He knew that was in his head. When you're laid there, doing nothing, day after day, those days can drag, and when days drag, they turn into longer days, and they can trick your mind.

Tricks of the mind were his biggest enemy. He had to try and resist them, try not to fall into a spiral of madness induced by his immobility.

Any bustle of noise outside the room perked him up. He didn't even care who it was who came to visit him anymore. Doctor. Nurse. Someone coming to torture him. Hell, he'd take a dinner date with the infected if it cured his solitude.

He never thought he'd hate being alone.

He'd made a habit out of it.

But two people had changed that. His two friends. Sadie. Donny.

And where were they now?

Probably trapped somewhere else within the building. If they were even alive.

The last time he'd seen Sadie, she was being tortured. Eugene Squire had restrained him and forced him to watch, forced him to be a voyeur until he gave up all he knew about Sadie's existence. Who she was. What she could do.

He'd said nothing.

But Gus knew Eugene was nobody's fool. They both knew Sadie was a remarkable girl; yet it had appeared at the time that Eugene hadn't learnt just how remarkable she was.

By now, that was probably no longer the case.

Then again, why else would Eugene keep Gus alive, except in hope that Gus might let on what he'd seen Sadie do? That he might spill his knowledge in hope of being put out of his misery?

After all, Sadie could be the key to everything. Whilst she appeared to be the daintiest, most fragile girl there could be, she most definitely was not. She hadn't the verbal ability of a human – in fact, there was very little human about her at all. She moved like a predator and attacked like a beast. Yet, there was something more than feral. She was like one of the undead, except she wasn't. She had survived her blood mixing with the infected without turning. The infected were strong and fast – but she was stronger and faster.

Her abilities surpassed theirs.

Gus knew there was something about the way she had reacted to their blood. He didn't know what it was, but he knew it was crucial – most of all, he knew he couldn't let Eugene know. Otherwise both he, and probably Sadie, would be killed.

She may be being tortured, but at least she was alive.

So, he said nothing.

He had to say nothing.

But the longer he said nothing, the longer he was left alone to wonder – does Eugene know?

And Donny. Where was Donny?

He hadn't seen him since they'd arrived. Since they had willingly walked through the doors, under the pretence that he was delivering Eugene's beloved daughter, whom he had saved from London – the hive of the undead. A pretence that turned out to be a lie.

That girl, that sweet, innocent little girl he'd rescued from London – Eugene had shot her in the head before Gus even had an inkling they were being betrayed.

All of it had been for nothing. The drive to London, getting into the quarantined city, fighting against thousands of the infected to get the girl out – *for nothing.*

Then again, no. It hadn't been for nothing. This was worse than nothing. Nothing would have been stuck in his old flat drinking himself to death. Nothing would be remaining in the peacefully ignorant life he'd been in before all of this happened.

No, he'd pretty happily take nothing at that moment, rather than having to lay there day after day, knowing nothing about where his friends were, or what was happening to them.

He lifted his head. Peered down his body. Still no leg.

Sometimes, he convinced himself it was because his leg had gone numb. That it was all a dream. That he'd wake up the next morning, look down and see it, relieved the dream wasn't true.

But it wasn't a dream.

It was gone. The bottom half of his right leg. From the knee downwards. All that was there was a stump.

It made sense, really. He had been shot in the leg years ago in Afghanistan, and the bullet had remained lodged in his calf. In the end, he'd had to reach into his calf and pull out the bullet to shoot the cannibal that was trying to kill him and Donny. He couldn't do such a thing and still expect the use of his leg.

How was he meant to get out of there?

Because, make no mistake about it – leg or no leg, he was

going to get out of there. He fully intended to make his escape. Any moment now, he was going to take his opportunity and leave.

Only, he'd been thinking that since the first moment he had been restrained to this bed. His wrists, waist, and only ankle, were fixed in place. The room was like a sterile hospital room; it smelt of cleaning products, its walls were a blank white, and every day, they seemed to close in on him a little bit more.

The door opened.

His only two regular visitors entered. They visited three times a day. Meal-times. And neither of them ever said a single word to him, however much he tried to lure conversation out of them.

The first man was a guard. He held a gun, a large machine gun – Gus couldn't make out the model – and he kept it fixed on Gus. Gus had read this guy's name badge, back before he stopped wearing it, and it had said his name was Corporal Krayton.

"Corporal," Gus declared. "So nice to see you again. How are we today? How's the wife? How's the kids?"

Krayton smirked a knowing smirk. A wide smirk, as if to say, *you're tied to the bed, I have the gun, why would I give a shit about how you taunt me?*

"Yeah, I've just been hanging out, you know, the usual," Gus continued. "Thought about going down the pub, but, you know, couldn't get these straps loose."

The second man was, Gus presumed, a doctor. A tall man with grey hair and stubble, his long, white coat trailing behind him. He sat on a chair beside Gus's bed, took out some food smushed into a container, and placed it on a teaspoon. He held the tea spoon to Gus's lips.

"This tastes like shit, you know that?" Gus said.

The doctor's expression didn't falter.

"Do I get to meet the chef? Say thank you? Or fuck you?

You know, whichever comes to mind."

The doctor didn't move. Just kept the food out, ready, waiting for him to eat.

He put his lips around the food. Took it into his mouth. Locked eyes with the doctor. Spat it at him.

Krayton stiffened his grip on his gun.

If the doctor was perturbed, he didn't show it. A flickering look of dismay passed his face, but it was gone in such an instant, Gus was sure he had imagined it.

Instead, the doctor took the food, stood, and walked out.

Keeping his gun aimed until the final moment, Krayton backed out of the room and shut the door. Gus heard it lock and he was alone again, alone with silence, and a fading, artificial light.

He wished he could wipe his mouth. When he'd spat out that shitty excuse for food, some had dribbled down his chin. He tried lifting his head and wiping his chin on his shoulder, but he couldn't manage it.

He laid his head back. Stared at the ceiling. That same, white, damn, fucking empty ceiling. That same pathetic, ridiculous, swiney ceiling. The same ceiling he'd stared at for minute after minute after hour after God-knows-how-long because there was no sodding clock in there and all he could do was just stare, stare, stare, stare at nothing, try not to go crazy, stare at the ceiling, look at the light, look at the absence of leg, look at the empty room, always empty, forever empty, always forever fucking empty.

Ah, alone again.

With myself.

"Hello, darkness, my old friend..." he sang, hoping for a laugh at the irony, the good choice of song. But he didn't even get an echo.

Just silence.

The same old silence.

Chapter Seven

Down the same blank sterile corridors, down the same neutral walls and marble floors, past the same men in lab coats and the women with glasses and pony tails pulled back, past the clipboards and the technology and the work – there was a darker side to the place that no one ever referred to. They all knew what they were doing was highly illegal and incredibly concerning. Everyone who worked there had a vague knowledge of what they were doing, but nothing specific. They were each a piece of the puzzle, and without all the pieces, they couldn't see the big picture – but they could still see their own piece of the puzzle and recognise what kind of piece it was. What is was contributing. What it could mean.

They were all sworn to an unspoken vow of secrecy.

And no one ever left.

They didn't even know if their families were alive. They didn't even know the extent of the post-apocalyptic world beyond the fences; there was no visual memory they had that told them what they needed to fear. But they smelled it when they opened a window. They heard it when they closed their eyes at night. They felt it when they had a momentary glance into another person's eyes. And, amongst all these thoughts and glances and concerns there was one unanimous comprehension: the world had changed. They didn't want to venture out there. Perhaps they liked convincing themselves they were prisoners – it gave them an excuse to not brave the changed world. It gave them reason to stay in their squalid rooms. To think that maybe, just maybe, what they were doing had a grander purpose.

Denial seems like a stupid reaction to the casual observer. But, when you are in a life-threatening situation, it is a genuine defence the human mind uses to protect you. People can't take the reality.

Ignorance is always easier.

And, if anyone chose not to be ignorant, to think that they may want to find their family, to stand up to Eugene Squire and General Boris Hayes and say that they did not want to continue as part of their operation – well, those people were few and far between. But one thing that was certain to anyone carrying out their work, whether they be a doctor, a physicist, a soldier, or just your regular, everyday torturer – those people who did object were never seen again.

Although, on occasion, a doctor, or physicist, or soldier, or torturer, would pause their work to glance out of the window at the distant fence and think, for a fleeting moment, that they had caught a glimpse of a missing friend's familiar face amongst the mass of infected – though they could never be sure.

But the lack of certainty was enough to keep them in line.

So the cycle went on. They carried out the tests Eugene wanted, carried out the actions Hayes demanded, went every which way to please their every need – then just hoped and prayed that it was for a better cause than they believed it was.

Many of them were even under the impression that they were going to cure the infection.

Quite the opposite.

Any murmur of conversation promptly halted as those familiar footsteps were heard tapping down the corridor. People recognised them anywhere. They were loud, like clown feet, and they belonged to the prime minister. Funny, for a man with such a tight-fisted rule, the terrifying sound of him approaching sounded a lot more like the scuffle of a rat running from a bigger rat. His shadow, getting ever closer, grew bigger, but never loomed. Yet, as he marched around the corner with his crew in tow, people's heads dropped and looked away. From behind their glass walls they continued in their laboratory, persisting in the tests he demanded they do, making sure he saw that they were hard at work.

In this instance, those footsteps stopped at the lift. Eugene swiped his card, entered a pin number, then selected to go down a floor – to the basement.

Only the few exclusive people with such an ID card and pin number could go to that floor.

As the doors opened, a very different hallway appeared. The brightly lit corridor and active laboratories were long forgotten down there, replaced by shadows and dark corners and distant dripping you couldn't place. A flickering orange light buzzed overhead, illuminating mossy cracks in the walls and stains on the floor.

Eugene walked to the room he required, swiped his card, indicated to his entourage to wait outside, and entered.

There she was.

He smiled and stood between the two armed guards with deadened expressions and focussed eyes. His smile spread, hands playfully on his hips, and he bent slightly over like a primary school teacher addressing a child.

"Ah, Sadie!" he sang. "And how are we today?"

She looked up at him and growled.

Her arms were above her head, a metal cuff around each wrist, attached to chains screwed deeply into the wall, and her restrained ankles were just the same. Her bleeding knees brushed the floor as she swayed under the lifeless clink of the rusty restraints, dangling from them, looking up to him with eyes that no longer had the energy to hate.

Her lip bled. Her eyes lulled. The naked body of a battered young woman was bruised and beaten, reddened and scarred from months of misery. Her skin clung to her bones like cling film around meat. Her ribs were clearly pronounced, her legs coated in a thick strip of brown hair, and her breasts, so dainty and wounded, small as two distinctly unnoticeable pyramids, were barely discernible from her fading body.

Despite the distant energy, vile detestation still surfaced in a growl, her response to Eugene's patronising question.

"Oh, I am sorry, where are my manners," Eugene continued. "Have you eaten?"

Her lip curled upwards into a snarl that was so weak it was barely audible. She wanted to leap forward and dig her teeth into his throat, rip out his oesophagus, bite off his face, turn him into a bloody, dead mess. But she lacked the energy or resolve. She had been in that position for too long. She had forgotten what liberty felt like.

"I could get something, if you would like? Some yoghurt? Some chicken?"

Her lip curled up again, revealing a bloody, broken tooth wayward from her bleeding gums.

"Maybe just the yoghurt then."

She growled, a longer growl, ending with an aggressive, "Argh!"

He shook his head. Sighed. She was feral when she was brought here, without a doubt. He was fascinated to find out what she was. Why the infection had affected her so differently to everyone else. He had thought – maybe she had become closer to what he had intended to create in the first place.

In that line of thinking, he had expected her to talk.

But she hadn't. She hadn't formed a word. Not a coherent syllable. And it was getting tiring.

He wanted to be done with this.

He wanted to give the lab what they needed to finish the project.

He wanted to just get on with it.

"Sadie, Sadie, Sadie," he said. "This is growing tiresome. I know you can speak. I know you can."

Another low-pitched growl.

"Oh, stop it. I know there are words in there. I know there are. I'm sure of it. Otherwise, how would you be... what you are? Eh? Tell me that, sunshine."

She mouthed something. Something that was barely a whisper. But it looked like words. Looked like something.

"What was that?" he asked, excited. Finally!

She did it again. He got closer.

"One more time." He turned his ear toward her and cupped it.

Then those three words she knew all too well grunted past her scabbed, cracked lips.

"Gus. Donny. Friend."

Eugene sighed.

"Oh, Sadie. That is not..." He clenched his fist. "That is not – that is – that is *not what I wanted!*"

He sent his fist soaring through Sadie's face.

She barely reacted. She was used to it. And he didn't pack much of a punch. In fact, it probably did more damage to his knuckles than it did to her bony face.

Still, he was perturbed. And she was the cause of it. And that did not make him happy.

"Sooner or later," he said, holding his wrist as he waited for the pain to subside, "I am no longer going to have a use for you."

He turned to the nearest guard.

"She doesn't move from this room unless she talks," he said, placing a key in the guard's pocket. "Bring her to me if she does."

He marched out of the room.

Leaving her alone.

With two armed guards for company.

Staring at her weary, diminishing, pathetic body.

She sniffed.

She could still smell them.

They were alive.

They had to be.

Chapter Eight

Detail was the emphasis. Inscrutable, minute, incontrovertible detail. That's what Doctor Janine Stanton had always believed. For within the detail is where she had made her best findings.

And this was the finding.

This was it.

And maybe, just maybe, after she announced it – the prime minister wouldn't need her anymore. He would let her go home. Be free.

Not that he'd ever said she wasn't free. Not explicitly, anyway. He had the calm demeanour of a wizened school teacher, the words of a politician, and the social appearance of the least-liked kid in class. It was just something in the way he spoke, the authority his commands held. He was the man in charge of the country. If he told you to do something and you didn't do it, well... What then?

There was hardly much of a government around to stop him.

A letter to the United Nations wouldn't get there. Partly because post doesn't really happen anymore, and partly because she wasn't even sure if they still existed.

But this, she was positive, was exceptionally good work. Her research prior to entering the compound had involved looking at many illnesses, picking them apart under the microscope. She had created vaccines, pharmaceutical pills to help keep colds away, and had even contributed to a large, extensive project attacking cancer – and, at the latter stages of her research, she had nearly found the cure; just oh, so nearly.

But then she was required elsewhere. Her government needed her, she was told, before she was taken in a van by the army, passing buildings on fire, hearing nothing but gunshots, passing deformed creatures who chased after them.

She soon got closer to those deformed creatures, spending most of her early days picking apart their corpses, scrutinising the infection, what it was doing, how it was spreading.

This was different to her previous work.

She wasn't looking for a vaccine. Or a cure.

She was looking for something else.

Something to make the infection... stronger.

"Good afternoon!" came that friendly voice that wasn't so friendly. Its cheeriness came with a loaded, sinister twinge that was hard to pinpoint, never mind articulate – but was there all the same. "Everyone hard at work, I see?"

Eugene saw her. Raised his eyebrows in greeting. His armed guard waited by the door as he approached.

"Doctor Janie Starton, I presume?" he said.

"It's Doctor Janine Stanton," she responded. "And please, call me Janine."

"Oh, I will. How goes it, Janine?"

"Well, sir. Really well, in fact."

His grin alighted.

"Wonderful. I trust you have some good news for me?"

"I think I've got what you wanted."

"Well, let's see it."

"First, before I show you, can I ask about my future? Should it be what you are wanting, I would very much like to–"

"Show. Me. It."

She felt like bowing. Curtseying. She didn't. She nodded fervently. She did consider, for a fleeting moment, refusing to show him anything until he listened; then her eyes drifted to the armed guard stood by the entrance. If she picked up a scalpel and lodged it into him, could she make it out alive?

No. Because she was a doctor. They were soldiers.

Such intermittent thoughts were pointlessly futile.

"Yes," she answered. "This way."

She led him to her work station and presented a microscope.

"What I am looking at, Janine?"

"Just look, please."

A brief scowl at her impatience flickered across his face. He peered into the microscope. He hovered there for a few seconds. His neck was exposed. Then he looked to Janine with eyes full of curiosity, like a child in a sweet shop, suddenly excited by the possibilities.

"Is this..." he asked. "Is this... really it?"

"I think so."

"You *think*?"

"I'm pretty certain. If you look at the cells – it's a cell of a human and of the infected. It's no longer attacking it."

"No, it's not."

"It's merging."

"And you did this from the blood of that feral girl?"

"I did, sir, yes."

He held his arms out into the air, as if he was about to embrace her in a hug, but just held them there, his grin getting wider, unnaturally so, taking up such a large portion of his face.

"Where were you eight months ago, eh?" he exclaimed, his voice full of bounce. "Where were you then when I needed this? This is... Ah, Janine. You are my saviour. This is exactly what I wanted. Exactly!"

"Could I – could I go home now?"

He raised a finger in the air and took a deep breath, feigning a look as if he was deeply considering this.

"Surely, Janine, surely, in good time."

"In good time?"

"Could you synthesise this?"

She looked to her research, then back to him. She didn't see why not. She would require more resources, but it could be done.

"Yes. I would need more people, but–"

"Then people you shall have! How soon could you have it done?"

"Give me enough people and I could have it this afternoon."

He clapped his hands together, hard, and waved his hands joyously in the air.

"Right, Janine, listen carefully. Here is what I want you to do..."

Chapter Nine

Singing to yourself passes the time. But does it make you sound crazy? Guess it does. To some people.

Then again, doesn't having an interior conversation with yourself make things worse...

Gus wasn't even sure if he was even speaking out loud anymore. Was that humming him? Was it an open vent? A fan? Someone else?

No, there was no one else with him. Who could it be?

How long had he been in there now?

Ooh, say, about, a few months...

Got to be realistic.

Can't be years. Haven't been fed enough.

Got to be months.

Surely.

But can you be positive?

Oh God, I'm doing it again.

He clenched his right fist. Pulled on his restraint. Felt it give a little bit more. Or did he?

Fact is, he'd been pulling at it for hours on end every day since he first arrived. Biding his time. Hoping it would give way eventually. Tugging on it a little bit each day; it's got to give some day, hasn't it? It may take forever, but surely – someday, right?

The bed frame looked to quiver. Fractionally. Buckle so minutely only a keen, in-tune mind would perceive it.

But that ain't me.

He was imagining it. It wasn't moving. Couldn't be.

It could.

Who knows.

The door buzzed. It opened once more. Corporal Krayton entered. His gun aimed, his eagle eyes looking through the viewfinder, focussing its target directly at Gus.

Gus smiled for him. Smile for the camera. For the audience. Give them a show.

"Well how do you do?" he asked. The intonations of his voice made him sound like the Mad Hatter. Which was strange, because he didn't know who the Madder Hatter was. *Guess it just feels right.*

He stopped pulling on his restraint. Stopped trying to make it buckle. What if Krayton saw the tiny movement?

Well. Yeah, go on. What if he saw it?

What then?

Krayton would have to react. Move a bit more. Interact. Pretend like Gus was a living organism, not an immobile object to be watched with a loaded weapon.

The doctor entered.

"No!" chimed Gus.

The doctor didn't react. Just carried on walking in with the tray.

"No, I said! Fuck off! Don't want you!"

Gus was so hungry. So, so hungry.

But also stubborn.

"You heard me, dick-face, beat it."

The doctor paused. Looked over his shoulder to Krayton.

As if he was going to give some indication as to what to do. He never did anything. Just stood there looking at Gus through a gun.

"What you looking at him for? Boy ain't got nothing about him. You ain't going to get shit from him."

The doctor looked back at Gus, then to Krayton.

"Ain't that right, soldier?"

Krayton shrugged at the doctor. A small gesture, but one very much noticed by Gus.

"Oh God, he reacts. There is someone lurking beneath."

The doctor left. Krayton went to go.

"When I kill you," Gus declared, "you're gon' look more like one of the infected than you do now, you stupid little prick."

Krayton paused. Held himself still in the doorway. Straightened his back.

"Oh my God, he reacts! He actually reacts! The fucking idiot zombie-head actually does something other than point a gun. Can you do anything other than point a gun?"

Krayton turned to Gus. With a knowing smirk. A dismissive shake of the head. A raise of his arms that reaffirmed who has the power.

"You got a wife, pretty boy?"

He raised his eyebrows and went to leave again.

"'Cause after I kill you, I'm goin' to fuck her."

He turned back.

"Yeah, that got you, didn't it? She a zombie yet? Cuz if so, I'll still fuck her walking, talking corpse."

Krayton raised his gun and rushed to the side of the bed, pointing it at Gus, but with more power, more aggression, holding it without the precision of a cool-minded sniper, but the rattled member of a shit gang.

"That got you, didn't it?"

"Just you wait," Krayton whispered, his voice low and husky, deeper than Gus was expecting. "Soon as Mr Squire gives the go-ahead, I'm gon' use this one bullet I got saved for you."

"But until then, you'll just have to behave. So, what is your wife's name? In fact, skip her name – if you could just write her address and phone number on the side there for me, I can do the rest."

Krayton smashed the butt of the gun into Gus's cranium.

Gus laughed. He thought that would hurt him? He had one fucking leg. That was like rubbing a bit of felt across his face, the inept idiot.

"You wan' know a secret?" Gus taunted.

"What?" Krayton spat, his face venomous, yet still incontrovertibly in control. After all, he wasn't the one fastened to a bed.

"Come closer, I got to whisper it."

Krayton leant lower.

"Closer..."

Krayton leant lower still.

In a sudden rush, Gus threw his head upwards to dig his teeth into Krayton's neck.

But he didn't dig his teeth into Krayton's neck.

He missed by inches.

His aim, his awareness, everything that made him a skilled fighter – it was way off. He was losing it. And Krayton found that hilarious. So much so, he fell to his knees laughing. Laughing at the idiocy that Gus Harvey thought he could fool him. The idiot who got himself captured and lost a leg – the washed-up, suicidal alcoholic who thought he was a bloody legend, held captive in a utility, with no knowledge of his friends' existence, thinking he could fool Krayton.

Gus watched the arsehole laugh. Watched him guffaw, screech, weep with convulsions of hilarity.

"I'll get you..." Gus said.

"No," Krayton said, standing up whilst wiping the tears from his cheeks, struggling to calm his hoots. "No, you won't."

Krayton left, still chuckling, and the door buzzed after him.

Alone again.

Hello, darkness, my old friend.

He tugged on his restraints. Looked to the headrest.

It didn't move.

But he'd get there eventually.

Surely.

Eventually.

Chapter Ten

Janine chewed the end of her pen.

It was a habit she used to hate in her students, in her brief time lecturing at the university whilst she acquired her PhD. She would look up, mid-talk, and notice it – a student with the end of a pen stuck in their mouth. Then the student would take it out and the pen would be mangled, squashed and condensed into a wreck barely recognisable as a writing utensil. Then she'd carry on. Detesting that individual student for no other reason than that they mildly chewed the end of their pen.

But, there she was, years later; her puzzlement reflected in arduous nibbling.

Then again, she was in a situation with overwhelming ethical complexities – she had the right to chew her pen. What reason did that student have? Exam deadlines? Relationship troubles?

Oh, what she'd give to only have the stress of an exam deadline or a difficult boyfriend. To resume such normalities of life, rather than being stuck between her patriotic duty and creating something potentially destructive on a worldwide scale.

Though, in all honestly, that student was probably dead now.

As was most of the country.

"Doctor Stanton?" a colleague said as they appeared at the doorway.

She shook her head, breaking herself out of a distant trance, and gave them her attention.

"Yes?"

"The subject is ready for you. Where do you want him?"

"Ah, I... Wherever."

"We have a private lab set up for you next door. Would you like him in there?"

Janine looked at this colleague. Was he thinking the same thoughts as her? Did he have the same hesitancies? Or was he also working on a broken promise he'd get to see his family someday?

Or was he as he appeared, and did in fact have no clue what was happening?

"Sure," Janine confirmed.

The guy nodded and left the room.

She waited. Sat alone in the silence of her tranquillity. Her own desk beside her, papers symmetrically arranged, paper tray perfectly organised, and the handle of her coffee cup pointed at a perfect right angle to the table.

She stood. Walked to the small window toward the top of the office, pushed herself onto her tiptoes, and looked out.

There they were. In the near distance. Surrounding the fences. Hundreds of them. Possibly more. There was always that distant growling, like a constant hum they'd grown used to. Then there was the smell that she didn't even notice anymore. But seeing them, in all their disgusting glory, clambering against each other, reaching for the fence, desperate for their next meal, was something else. It was a different experience entirely.

Her colleague's face appeared at the door once more.

"He's ready for you, Doctor."

"Is he strapped down?"

"Yes."

"Then leave him be. I'll be in in a moment."

"Right you are."

The guy left.

Her subject awaited.

That poor, poor subject.

Did he have any idea? Did he know what was about to happen? Was he a willing volunteer, a delusional madman, or a manipulated prisoner?

Whatever he was, he was just another tool of Eugene Squire. Something beaten by the marvellous General Boris Hayes – and, let's face it, who hasn't taken a beating from him every now and then?

Shortly after she had started there, he'd made a pass at her. Whilst his wife was sleeping in his room. She'd rejected him. He hadn't liked it. She'd learnt what kind of man he was.

She stood. Sighed. Wiped her hands over her face.

I could do with a cigarette.

Not that she'd ever had one. She'd just heard it calmed nerves. And she could do with whatever she could get.

She stepped out of the room. Looked down the corridor. Sterile. Clean. Blank.

Two armed guards stood outside her private lab.

Of course they did.

She closed her eyes. Dropped her head.

Why was she doing this?

She could refuse.

And what then?

Some other genius would take her place, and she would be left to fend for herself in the herd of infected battering at the fences.

No. It was up to her.

She walked weakly down the corridor. It was only a few paces, but she felt her knees buckle, her legs wobble like jelly. Already she could feel her blouse sticking to her body, stuck to her by sweat. She had a hot flush. Her belly lurched.

She needed to get a grip.

Control yourself.

She caught sight of her own reflection in the glass walls of the passing laboratories. She looked like hell. Maybe it was a glimpse of what she'd look like after she was thrown into the horde outside for refusing to do her job.

Her job.

Jobs have pay checks.

What did she have?

My life.

And she guessed that would have to do.

She gripped the door handle too hard. Softening her push, she opened the door, but its weight held itself against her. She pushed harder and stumbled in. She closed the door and locked it.

There he was.

The subject.

Sat on a chair in the middle of the room. Her equipment had been set up on tables around him, every utensil she'd need, whether it be for analytical, surgical, or synthetical purposes, she need never leave this room.

He looked young. Younger than she expected. Though she wasn't sure what she had expected. His hair looked scruffy, like it had been poorly styled into a bed head – a popular style boys used to have when she was still at school and dating. His face was bruised. His bony arms, peeping out of his white patient's outfit, clutched the side of the chair.

His face was red.

He was breathing erratically.

But he didn't say anything. For some reason, he looked like

he couldn't. Like there was something behind his eyes, or in his mind, irreparable damage that had scarred his perceptions. Whatever it was, something was keeping him still, yet petrified, yet cooperative.

"Hello," Janine said, unsure what she was saying. "My name is Doctor Janine Stanton. Do you understand what is going to be happening to you?"

His eyes widened. Like his eyelids were being pulled apart. Pure terror. Yet completely docile. Aggressively submissive.

"What is your name?"

His mouth didn't open. It remained tightly closed.

She picked up his chart.

"Well, it doesn't say your name here."

She flipped through a few pages, then she saw it. His name, from before.

"Well, I guess I'll just call you by this previous name, then," she said.

She held her eyes over him. Fixed. Surveying his reactions.

She'd better get to work. She didn't have long.

"Right, shall we get started then, Donny?"

FIVE DAYS LATER

Chapter Eleven

Rage is something shared across most species.

It's more than annoyance, or anger, or hostility. It's something that starts inside and burns its way through the acidity of your stomach, blackens your blood, scorches through your nervous system, coasting along on its own adrenaline.

It's something you can recognise in yourself, but usually not until long after it's started. For a human, it's something you can consciously acknowledge, and either control, harness, or release.

For an animal, it's not words; it's a familiar feeling. Not something one knows through internal awareness, but something one is still unmistakably aware of. Like an old friend that causes you nothing but misery, but you shake their hand nonetheless, welcome them into your life with their sledgehammer and let them batter away at everything you've built.

For Sadie, this rage had grown far stronger than she knew by the time she became aware.

Her thoughts, which weren't as coherent as yours or mine in the first place, were now obscured with a vision of wrath. They were marked with a bloody swipe of a claw, scarring her perceptions, wounding her thoughts.

Her lip curled into the snarl first.

Those two armed guards. Stood at ease on the opposite side of the room – but the room was such a box, they were still close enough to taste. Close enough to smell.

She sniffed.

She still had Donny's scent. She still had Gus's scent. She knew they were alive.

But that thought was buried deep within her mind.

It was only now that humiliation was dawning on her. Her body was cold. Her constant aches thawed, her bones still, her muscles twitching. Her fingers flexed, like a corpse awakening, like a body coming back to life.

Electricity rode along the synapses of her brain with a trail of fire behind them.

Her head lifted.

Her snarl echoed.

They looked at her. Those two armed bastards, they looked at her. Eyebrows gently tweaking. Becoming alert to danger.

Before they knew anything, her rage had intensified.

She was never meant to be held against a wall. Restraints could never contain someone of her ability. It was a foolish situation for all involved.

She swiped her arms downwards, pulling on her chains. In the end, it didn't take too much to free herself; the rage did it for her. She wrenched the stones attached to the other end of the chains from the wall, collapsed them against the floor in a dusty mist, smashing them into a hundred rocks.

One leg kicked.

The other leg kicked.

An armed guard took aim. Shot her in the leg.

She looked down.

An open wound emerged atop the bruises. Through some

miraculous miracle – at least, it seemed miraculous to the guard – the open wound swelled up and shut, leaving another scar for her broken canvas.

Did they not know what she was?

What she could do?

The infected couldn't be stopped via a shot in the leg.

She smiled at them. Not a welcoming smile, or a sympathetic smile, or even a knowing smile – no, this was a smile of pure arrogance. Rage entwined with a realisation of what she was actually capable of. An awareness of what she could realistically do to her captors.

The armed guards looked at each other. As if silently communicating, they lifted their guns and prepared to fire.

Their fingers never got close enough to their triggers.

Her arms were still in the cuffs, still attached to the chain, which was still attached to a small clump of stone. She lifted the right chain and swung it overhead like a lasso, twirling it, spinning until it gathered speed. She brought it around in a full circle, taking it to the first guard's cheek, and swiping his head clean off his body.

She lifted her left hand up and lunged the chain forward, sending the remaining stone through the far wall – the other guard's head betwixt the two.

She let the restraints drop. Stood on the stone loosely dangling from her right arm. Pulled at her chains, tried to wrench her reddened wrist free, but there was no way to do this without breaking her wrist.

Then she remembered what Eugene had placed in the guard's pocket. From its concealment it glistened. She wasn't entirely sure what it was, but she knew what it could do. She clutched the key and placed it in her restraints and released her hands, followed by her ankles.

For the first time in so long, she could move.

She could run again.

She was unleashed.

She sniffed.

Donny was close. He was so close.

She scampered out of the door, running on her arms and legs.

As she emerged into the corridor, a man was approaching with a gun, arriving to assess the commotion.

Before he could pull the trigger, she pounced, using the wall as a stepping stone and landing atop his shoulders. She sunk her teeth deep into his gullet, weakening his tendons. With a pull of her arm, she ripped the man's head clean off.

She looked up.

More armed guards entered the corridor.

The rage thrust into her heart, making it beat, beat faster, pound, ready.

She prepared her claws.

They prepared their guns.

She smiled pitifully. They had no idea.

Chapter Twelve

The breeze was gentle, carrying a splash of distant rain.

Eugene relished it. Enjoyed it.

He'd earnt it.

Hayes entered the roof, walked to Eugene, and stood by his side.

They remained in a moment of triumphant silence, standing atop the compound, watching the scenes below.

At the edge of the buildings was a narrow circle of green. Beyond that, fences. Fences struggling under the weight. Fences that weren't meant to take this kind of force. Against them, hundreds, possibly thousands, of the infected, pushing. They could hear, smell, possibly even taste the flesh on the air – inside these buildings was enough food for all of them. An all you can eat buffet without the manners. It would be chaos for humans – but perfection for the undead.

"So?" Eugene prompted. "Conclusion?"

"The subject is prepared," Hayes replied. "The doctor did a magnificent job on him. She should be commended."

"Oh, she will. I mean, not in her lifetime – but someday.

History books are written by those who win, Boris. That means this history will be written by me. By us. And we will write this as a great victory – not in the way they would write it."

"All history is told from a particular point of view," Hayes pointed out. "My time in Iraq, where they saw *us* as the enemy, taught me that."

"And who's the enemy now?"

They both grinned. A gloating, over-sure, but not undeserved grin.

"I always enjoy a cigar at times like this," Eugene said. "Would you care for one?"

"I would."

Eugene took out a small, black box. He opened it, took a cigar, and offered one to Hayes. They lit them, then stood there, puffing on them, pushing smoke into the sky.

"Beautiful," Hayes declared.

"They are Elie Bleu Che, soaked in Remy Martin cognac – a bottle of which is fine and tasty, and lives in my office. An amateur would look at them and just see a humidor."

"Well, I don't know what that means, but they're fucking good."

"Oh, aren't they?"

A noise approached. Then a small object. As it grew bigger, the sound of the propeller became recognisable, and the helicopter came into view.

"This ours?" Hayes asked.

"Of course."

They took a few more intakes of success, then patted their cigars out as the helicopter made its descent.

"And the AGA?" Eugene said.

"Sorted. The trap is expected to happen in the next few days."

"Wonderful. Just, wonderful."

The helicopter landed.

"Right, time to leave," Eugene declared. "Subject is prepared, trap is set. I'd say our work is done, wouldn't you?"

"Yes, I would."

"Lovely. You have the green light, General. End it all. Leave no survivors. No one can know of our research."

"Roger."

Eugene directed himself toward the helicopter. As he did, Hayes withdrew a single trigger. He pulled it, and almost immediately, the detonations started. In quick succession, around the base of the fence, small bursts of explosions punched out the base of the only defence between the compound and the hungry undead.

The fence went down.

The infected stormed through, scrambling forward, fighting against each other. It took seconds for them to enter the building.

The screams started.

Hayes joined Eugene in the helicopter, which floated them away.

Chapter Thirteen

The sturdy fences folded like they were nothing. A few explosives in their foundations and they crumbled beneath the weight of a thousand feet.

Some of them fell. They were trampled on, too.

It was too much. They could taste it on the air, coming ever closer, the freshness of living flesh, the way that people always smelt so... alive. It was appetising. An appetizer, main, and dessert, all rolled into one epic combination.

Their teeth chattered so hard it knocked some wayward teeth down their throats. It didn't matter, they didn't choke.

Soil sludged and sank beneath their soggy feet, the ground losing its sturdiness, the grass only planted months ago, the soil wet from the weather, not ready for such force.

They reached the building.

The people tried to close the door. Tried to lock them out.

They just smashed right through the window. Fell over each other in their eagerness to enter. The doors gave way under the force of multiple bombarding bodies, row after row after row after row of them, disorganised, heavy. The weakest of them were flattened. They were left behind. The rest were hungrier. They wanted it more.

The humans ran.

But they couldn't run fast enough.

An armed guard tried to fight. He stopped, turned, and fired his weapon. Foolish boy, he missed their heads. He was dove upon and taken down, forced to lie in submission as they surrounded him, each feeding on a different part; his toes, his feet, his inside-out stomach, his screaming mouth exposing his helpless tongue, his wide, terrified eyes vulnerable to sharp nails. It took seconds for him to be drawn and quartered, then quartered again, then spread across the walls until he was finished with and their hunger wasn't satisfied, and they wanted more.

The spread like a flood. Once one room was full they spread through the corridor to the next, to the next, to the next.

Some people tried to run. Tried to make it to the window; a window too small for a dog to fit through, but that's what you do, isn't it – take any farfetched possibility of survival you can cling to. No one wants to die. Well, most people don't. So you try. Latch onto any bit of hope.

Then you turn and accept your fate, or continue in denial.

Some took scalpels, letter openers, dinner forks, anything they could to kill themselves so they were spared the pain of having to be eaten alive.

Some didn't get the chance.

The infected were fast. So fast. Quicker than your average leopard; could easily outrun a motorbike. And always hungry. Starving. Eating quickly didn't make them sick, didn't spoil their appetite. They could go on longer, they could go for more.

Doctors. Prisoners. Governors. Servants. Everyone was the same. All of them reluctantly accepting the same fate.

That was the ground floor. They had plenty of floors to go

up and down, and they found them, through the stairs, through the lifts where they tried to escape.

The floor above was lined with offices. People working heard the commotion. Some dove out of the window, only to find no escape. Some hid under desks, because they were idiots. Some prayed.

Prayed.

To whom?

A God who would allow this?

What did he give a shit?

One man stood. Straightened his tie. Closed his eyes. Took it like a man. He'd been expecting it – in fact, he'd been waiting for it. Seeing them at the fences all day. Knowing he was doing shitty work for a government that didn't care anymore.

He lost his thumb first. Bitten clean off by a creature whose mouth was already stained with blood. Then another took his arm, another latched onto his nose and tugged at it. It was really on there, so it took a few tugs, but it got it, barely chewed, swallowed it in one.

One man looked out the window and saw a helicopter disappear into the distance. He knew who it was. He went to say, "Selfish son of a bitch," but he only managed to get "Sel–" out before he was cut short.

Then there was the next floor down.

The laboratories.

Where Doctor Janine Stanton had heard the commotion.

She looked at her subject. He clenched his fists.

Maybe she should let him die.

Maybe she should let herself die.

No. She'd bide her time. As best she could.

She shut the door. Went to lock it.

The lock was broken.

She stood back.

The subject did nothing. Was he even thinking? Aware as to what was going on?

She bowed her head. Closed her eyes. She would have to wait this out. Hope no one ran in seeking refuge. Hope the infected couldn't open doors. Hope they couldn't smell her.

Hope.

Because that's all she could do.

Then she heard it. A tapping. Something was there. Something not like the infected.

Then it growled.

The infected didn't growl.

She had no idea who it–

She looked to her subject. To her research. To the blood she had used to synthesise what Eugene had needed.

The girl whose blood she'd used. Looking for her friend.

It must be.

She'd let the girl in. She would. But not yet.

First, she would go to her webcam and complete her fifth and final journal entry.

The most important thing was that her research was known.

That the truth was known.

Chapter Fourteen

Even before the gentle stream of screams had entered his mind, Gus knew what was happening. He recognised it.

He'd been to London, remember.

Under false pretences dictated to him by Eugene Squire, he'd braced the hive of the undead in the quarantined central city of the United Kingdom. He'd entered, rescued a girl he was led to believe was Eugene's daughter, and escaped whilst being chased by thousands.

He'd seen it. The masses of them, together, like a pit of hunger, reaching out for any sign of food. He'd smelt the potent death, so large and so big it filled his lungs, grew so strong, grew faint as he began to no longer recognise it anymore.

This was no different.

Following the rumble was the shake of the building as hundreds of them pounded the walls, battering their skulls against the doors, helplessly seeking a way in.

He knew he had minutes until they got to him. If that.

What was he supposed to do? He was immobile. He hadn't

moved from this position in months. And even if he did get up, he had one leg.

Then he remembered.

Sadie. Donny.

What if they were restrained just the same?

Helpless. Humiliated. Dead upon confrontation with the infected.

If this bed frame was going to buckle, now was the time. He'd been wearing on it hour after hour, day after day. He'd sworn he'd seen it shift, seen it shake, he was sure of it – but then the next moment it would be rigid, immovable.

Was he imagining things?

Maybe that's what had happened. Hallucinations of a mind spiralling into insanity. The drugs they pumped through him to numb the pain of the amputation must have been strong. Maybe they did something to him. Or, maybe it was just the lengthy monotony of staying there in a stationary stance. Boredom tampers with your mind, manipulates what you see, what you perceive. Constant emptiness and vacancy and removal from life – the consequences such desolation have on a feeble mind can be irreparable.

But my mind ain't feeble.

Pull. Pull. All the energy he had. He wasn't doing this subtly anymore, no attempt to do it without being noticed. So what if they noticed him? Right now, those guards outside his room – they had bigger issues.

The bed frame wobbled.

He saw it. It was real.

His arm moved with it. Moved further than it normally could.

The frame wobbled again.

Maybe!

Heavy stomps battered up a nearby staircase, the sound travelling closer. They were coming. They were done with the ground floor, but not done completely; no, there was plenty more food available. And they were going to find their food – very, very soon.

Pull.

A bigger wobble.

This could work.

Bloody hell, this could work.

The doors at the far end of the corridor. Their creak was unmistakable. Every time he heard it, his heart leapt, hopeful it was food, or Sadie, or Donny, or something.

Except now, it was different.

It wasn't a gentle creak. It wasn't a mild creak.

It was a slam. A whack. Then a skid as the door was taken off its hinges and scraped along the wall of the corridor.

Their snarls and snapping and sadistic salutations grew deafening.

Pull.

The bed frame dislodged.

Pull. Harder, this time. More. All the strength he had. The muscle ached from lack of use, but he had to persevere, he'd had worse than this, far worse. He was a war hero, for Christ's sake. A long time ago, but he was. He'd fed off scraps as his comrades died around him.

His wife. His child. Mauled to death. In front of him. The image scarred upon his retina.

If he could overcome that, he could overcome this.

A large swing of his arm took the bed frame off.

His arm was loose.

He held his hand out before him. Astonished. As if he'd never seen it before. His palm rough. His skin coarse. His freedom visible.

Screams outside the room.

He lifted the rest of the bed frame off and freed his other

arm. Then, using the strength of both arms, he pulled the bottom frame of the bed away and freed his remaining ankle.

The handcuffs were still fixed to his joints. But they were detached. Liberated.

Jesus, I'm fucking free!

He went to stand and fell hard onto the solid marble floor below.

Every muscle that he hadn't used ached. His arms that lifted him up, his waist that rotated, his shoulders, every flex was a barrage of pain.

He went to stand up again. Slipped.

He'd forgotten.

Just one leg now.

How could he forget?

Looking down, the vacant leg was blaringly obvious. That leg's presence hadn't meant anything to him before, but now its absence was unmistakably clear. He could feel nothing below his knee. A stump where his nerves ended. Complete emptiness. A hollow nothing.

Get a grip.

He couldn't dwell on it. Not now. This was about survival. He could cry over spilt milk later.

Using the bed, he pulled himself upwards, used it for leverage and support, using the floor to push him up, and he steadied himself, unbalanced but upright, leaning against the bed.

He continued to use its support as he hopped toward the door.

He shifted his body weight from the bed to the wall. Steadying himself. Falling, then regaining stability.

He made his way to the door. With great difficulty, but he made it.

He opened it.

Corporal Krayton turned and looked Gus in the eyes. A

boyish look, his eyebrows raised, like he was caught at a bad moment doing something naughty. Before Gus could understand why, it was spelled out for him.

One of the infected dove upon Krayton, took him to the ground and bit the bastard's ear off. Before the next few infected were upon Krayton, displacing his limbs and insides, Gus had slammed the door shut.

He locked it from the inside. Put one hand against the wall as he pulled a chair closer, placing it against the door. Then doing the same with the bed. Balancing. Falling. Stumbling. But doing it. Pulling the bed closer, the chair, barricading himself in.

The cowardly way.

But what else could he do?

If he went outside that room, hopping against the hundreds storming down the corridor, he was dead. He was no use to anybody dead.

Then again, he was no use to anybody anyway.

He collapsed, falling down the wall, landing painfully on his arse; he'd been laid down for so long, it had been a while since he'd sat.

The door moved. Again. A few prods, shaking it.

Then it pounded. Bumped. Moved the bed across the room under the ferocity.

They could smell him.

And he had nowhere to go.

Chapter Fifteen

A dozen of the infected and their dislodged throats lay vacantly at Sadie's feet.

Her fingers were blemished with blood. It stuck off her hand in splodges like dried glue. Her hair was drenched in it, her skin marked, her eyes boasting a demented focus on the door ahead. Her naked body was dressed in robes of violence, covered from head to toe in the masses she'd defeated.

She could smell him. Behind the door.

And someone else. There was someone with him.

She drummed her fingernails against the door. Allowed them to slow rat-a-tat a tuneless, ominous sequence of four solid marks.

The door was already open.

There stood a woman. She recognised the coat. It was what the doctors wore. The doctors who had prodded and probed her, stuck needles in her, held her down, ignored her screams. Everything she had experienced made her despise that coat.

"Are you..." the woman said. "Are you... her?"

Sadie twisted her head.

She wasn't like other girls.

Other girls communicated. Thought in more than brief words and venomous actions. Acted without such a ruthless scorn.

"My name is Doctor Janine Stanton," the woman said.

Sadie lifted her head, her greasy hair drooping over her lethal eyes. Between the threads of her thick locks, she saw him. Sitting. Alone.

Donny.

His hands restrained.

Fixed to the chair.

Like she had been.

Was that what this woman was doing to him?

Sadie's finger nails dug into her palms.

"Listen," the woman said. "I don't want to hurt you."

The woman lifted her hand out. Stroked the hair out of Sadie's face. Revealing the wrathful emptiness that lurked behind her eyes.

Doctor Janine Stanton was doing this as a sign of affection.

Sadie didn't understand that.

Every arm that had been reached out to her wearing that coat had been to hurt her. Humiliate her. Ignore her cries.

No more.

Sadie would have no more.

"Look, I know who–"

Janine interrupted herself with tormented screams.

Sadie's canines went clean through the doctor's arm.

Janine tried to tug her arm from Sadie's teeth, tried to pull, but that only weakened the tendons of her arm that Sadie had lodged in her jaw. She'd latched on like a dog on a bone or a luscious slab of meat, wriggling her head, wondering why this arm didn't break as easily as those others, the ones with the pale faces, but persevered anyway, kept biting, until she eventually tore her head backwards, taking part of the arm off with her.

But it wasn't clean. Fractions of bone and muscle still clung to Janine's elbow like stubborn pieces of spaghetti.

Before Janine could even acknowledge the agony, Sadie jumped, took her to the floor, bit into the throat, latched on, tore, ripped, tugged at her. Then her face. Then her throat again, on the other side. Again. Until the doctor didn't move anymore. Until she was a helpless puddle of blood. Ripping, tearing, pulling away.

Crouched over the corpse, Sadie lifted her head with a sudden memory of urgency.

"Donny," she grunted. One of the few words she could. "Donny. Friend."

His head slowly rotated. His eyes were elsewhere. His face was nothing.

She bit and ripped off his restraints, then lifted her hand and beckoned him.

"Come."

He stood robotically. Looked at her. Recognition not appearing on his face. Yet he was obedient. Like he was doing his duty.

Sadie couldn't understand.

Why was he acting like this?

"Donny."

Nothing.

"Friend," she reminded him.

He took a few steps toward her.

"Where do we go?" he asked.

She motioned for him to follow.

The made their way toward the horde. Sadie readied herself to fight, to defend Donny, to keep himself.

But she needn't.

The horde made no advances on Donny. In fact, they went nowhere near him. It was like they didn't want to taste him. He was diseased. Or something else. They just parted at the sight of him.

Sadie didn't care.

She had Gus's scent, and she had Donny.

She was half way there.

Chapter Sixteen

The bed abrasively battered the door, beating against the bombardment of bodies bashing against it.

Gus's strength wasn't enough. He was one man. One one-legged man, who hadn't even started to understand what that meant yet.

He crawled to the other side of the bed he'd barricaded against the door and he pushed against it, resisting as much as he could. But he had no leverage. Nothing for him to push against.

Snarls entered the room. The door ajar, multiple arms reaching in, scabby hands with missing fingers, ragged clothes hanging from bony bodies. One of them got their face in, their nose sniffing with eager delight. They could smell him. New flesh. Living flesh.

He wondered what he smelt like.

Then he cursed that such a thing may be his dying thought.

It must have been like a good steak was to him. Luring him in with its juices, its crisp coating, its luscious meat with the blood oozing out – and right then, Gus realised how hungry he was.

He ducked down behind the bed.

Like that was going to do anything.

Sure, the bed would hide him from a mass of the undead. They could smell him down the corridor, but no, the bed, that's what would do it.

He chuckled to himself.

Funny, really. For six months following his family's death he was so keen to die. He'd almost done it. He'd had the pills in his mouth, ready to leave it all behind.

Then something changed it.

Someone.

Two someones, in fact.

He wondered if those two friends he'd somehow managed to attain were even still alive amid the chaos of the compound.

He closed his eyes. Pictured his wife's face. Skin so soft. Eyes so pure. And his daughter. So keen. So eager to please him.

He didn't believe in heaven. Nor did he believe in hell. So he didn't realistically, in his heart, think he would ever be reunited with them. That he'd ever see them again.

But, just for a second, he allowed himself to believe. Thought about what he'd say to them. Thought about placing his lips on hers one more time.

He understood why people believed in the afterlife, it just seemed like bullshit to him. Think about all the stars in the sky, the vast planets out there, the amount of life forms that must exist. To believe that there is a specific place after death for humans is to believe that humans are far more significant than they are. In the grand scheme of things, people are just dust on the sleeve of a greater being. God, if he existed, didn't intervene because people didn't really matter. Because people were nothing. To the grander universes and solar systems out there, they were an ant. No, less. They were barely even a microbe.

Gus opened his eyes.

Something had changed.

He'd gotten lost in thought, readied himself for inevitability. Somehow, he'd failed to reason.

The bed wasn't pushing against his back anymore. The growls were gone. He turned around, and the arms were gone too.

But something else was battering against the door. Trying to open it.

He instinctively moved out of the way, so that whatever it was could punch the door against the bed and enter. He was cautious, but this didn't feel like one of the infected. It felt like...

"Oh, God."

He couldn't believe it.

It couldn't be.

Standing in the open door, bodies on the floor behind her feet, a pile of infected left discarded and destroyed, she stood. Her feral face, her bare, wounded body, and her eyes – those eyes that said to so many that she was an animal, but to him, said that she was a scared girl. Those eyes that reminded him of his daughter. They looked back, wounded.

His instinct was that he'd let her down. Wherever she'd been, she'd been stripped, tortured, hurt. He'd been tied to a bed, big fucking deal – by the look of her, she'd been torn apart day after day.

He used the bed to bring himself to his foot. Balanced himself on it. Looked at her full of solemn despair.

She had been let down. She had. And he hadn't even thought it. He hadn't even...

Her grim frown curved upwards. A mischievous smile accompanied a glint in the eye. As Gus helplessly smiled, she ran into his chest and he enveloped her in his arms.

"Oh, Sadie," he whimpered. "I'm so, so sorry."

From the doorway, another familiar face.

"Donny!" Gus yelped. He lifted his arm out as an indication for Donny to come into the hug as well.

Donny didn't move.

His face didn't move.

Gus's friend, so comical, so playful – and annoyingly so – stood there, with an expression Gus couldn't even fathom. He didn't even look like Donny; Gus had to look twice. The way he held himself, it was like he was void of feeling, void of recognition.

"Donny, what's the matter?" Gus asked.

Donny didn't change expression. His neutrality punched through the tension, alerting Gus.

What had they done to him?

"Hey, Donny, mate," Gus said, being decisive. "Could you get some clothes off one of the bodies, yeah? Perhaps, one with no blood on it, if it's possible. Something to cover Sadie up 'til we find something better."

Donny's eyes lingered on Gus for a moment then he turned, his body hunched without purpose, and he retreated back into the corridor.

Gus turned to Sadie.

"What's up with him?"

Sadie looked perplexed.

Oh, yeah. She's feral. Can't understand me.

"Donny okay?" he tried. "Donny – he okay?"

Sadie shrugged.

Gus nodded. He wasn't sure why, but he nodded.

"What did they do to you?" Gus asked, filled with compassion, his chest hurting at the thought of the pain she must have endured.

Sadie's head dropped.

"Hey," Gus said, lifting her chin up. "It's okay. We're all together now, we'll be fine. Yeah?"

Donny returned and handed a bunch of clothes to Sadie as

if he was handing her a bomb only she could dismantle. He kept his distance and backed away as soon as she'd taken them.

As she dressed, Gus kept his eyes on Donny, who stared absently at the wall.

Was Donny mad at him? Was it because Gus hadn't done anything to save him? Or was it because they had messed him up that badly?

In which case, did they need to worry about what he was going to do? Was he going to act out, put them in danger somehow?

No. Gus knew Donny. Donny, whom he'd literally given a leg to save. Donny knew what Gus would do for him, what he had done for him. There was something else.

Gus was snapped out of his contemplation by Sadie, who was standing by the door, ready to go.

"Donny, help me walk," Gus requested.

Donny looked at Gus, paused, then walked over and put an arm around his back. He even managed to do that in a cold manner, such a lack of caring or concern for the friend he was doing it to.

"What's up with you, man?" Gus whispered to him as Donny helped him to the door.

"Nothing," Donny blankly replied. "Nothing is wrong."

"I don't know, you seem pissed. I'm sorry I didn't get to you to save you, if that's what it is, I know they must have done some messed-up shit to you. They did it to me, and Sadie too, and–"

"Nothing is wrong. Let's just get out of here."

Gus nodded.

Fine. Maybe it would take time. Whatever had happened to them all, they were going to have to recover. First thing to do was get out, then they could deal with it.

"Okay, Sadie," Gus said as Donny helped him into the corridor. "Do your thing."

More infected emerged from the rooms opposite, the announcement of fresh blood approaching.

Sadie went to attack.

She didn't need to.

They all stopped. Dormant. Unmoving. Just looked at them.

Or, rather, looked at Donny.

"What the fuck..." Gus muttered.

Chapter Seventeen

The compound disappeared into the distance behind them, obscured by the high trees of the forest.

"Man, that really was in the middle of nowhere," Gus said, keeping his arm around Donny.

Sadie kept a few paces ahead, remaining cautious, keeping a lookout. Making sure there were no surprises.

But she needn't have.

None of the infected had attacked them. None of them at all. They had stood aside and let them walk out.

Gus was appreciative, but also sceptical.

Why?

How?

And, you know – *what the fuck?*

Donny didn't react.

He did as he should. Kept Gus steady. Kept his one leg moving. Helping him slowly meander away. Further away. Away from the compound. Away from what had been their home.

There was no home anymore.

Donny looked at Sadie. Far ahead. Running with a stutter.

Moving with jolts that made him wary. She could do anything at any moment.

Gus next to him. Useless.

Donny remembered Gus. Gus used to be so much more. Gus had been a soldier, or something. Someone who'd fought in wars.

What else was there to know about Gus really?

"Over there," Gus said, pointing out a broken-down house, one that looked like it had been burnt-out long ago. "That can be our shelter tonight. It's getting dark, we need to rest."

Sadie rushed ahead to the house. Checked it out.

Donny helped Gus up the messy lawn. For a big, bulky guy, Gus felt weightless. Like hollow air. So when Donny helped Gus to a sitting position on the splintered floor of their night's accommodation, it wasn't much relief.

"I'll take first watch," Gus proposed. "Sadie, if you want to–"

"I don't want to sleep," Donny interrupted. "I'll take watch."

"Okay, if you wake us up in four hours, then–"

"No. I'll watch all night. I've slept enough."

An uncomfortable silence lingered. Donny could tell Gus was unsure.

"Are you positive, mate? I mean, you've been through a lot."

"I'll be awake anyway. I don't want to sleep."

"We've had a tough run, you need to rest, gather your energy–"

"I don't need to gather any energy. I will be fine. Stop worrying."

Gus glanced to Sadie, who'd already curled up in the corner.

"If you're sure."

"Yes. I'm sure. Go to sleep."

Gus laid down. Slumped onto his back.

Donny stood at the window, looking out, into the dark settling upon the night. It was quiet. He could still feel Gus's eyes on him. Still watching him. Figuring him out.

Donny couldn't see the compound anymore.

It had disappeared.

They were on their own.

No.

He was on his own.

They were with him.

The Journal of Doctor Janine Stanton

Day 1

Transcript from webcam journal by Janine Stanton, first entry

I feel apprehensive. I guess that's natural. This is big, right?

I don't even know if I should be doing what I'm doing. But, let it be known in case this entry becomes public record, I am doing as requested by the prime minister, Eugene Squire. I am doing my duty.

Right?

I mean, if the prime minister asks you to do something – you do it.

The subject's name is Donny Jevon. Or, it was, I suppose. For now, I am just supposed to call him the subject. We are always reminded to distance ourselves from the subjects of our experiments, only, before, I was distancing myself from rats, or mice, once even a monkey.

Never from a human.

(pauses)

The first injection went smoothly, but to no avail.

TEST SYNTHESIS #1

28% blood of mutation

3% blood of infected
10% blood of subject
18% ketorolac
15% cortisone
26% water

I LEFT THE BLOOD OF THE MUTATION, INFECTED AND SUBJECT together overnight to combine and mix together, giving it time to, you know, become one, as it were. When I tested the reaction between the doses under the microscope, there was little reaction, but the infected hadn't taken over the subject with the mutation present, so I was not prepared to go ahead and shove loads of crazy stuff into this guy's – the subject's, sorry – body, without starting on a low dose.

It's just being cautious, and all that. I know Mr Squire wants this quickly, but I – I – I have to do my job, I guess. And this is no good to the prime minister if the subject is dead.

It's no good to my chances of survival either. I dread to think–

(pauses)

Anyway.

I added ketorolac to the mixture to remove any pain that may result, and cortisone to help with any muscle growth. I mixed this with water to dilute it, help it enter his bloodstream, but I fear this may have diluted it too much.

Upon initial injection, subject does little to react. Barely even notices when I stick the needle in his arm.

His face twitches, but his eyes don't move. It's chilling, how he stays so still.

I don't know what they've done to him.

I don't know if I want to know what they've...

I'm aware he saw Doctor Emma Saul. I've spoken to her a few times, and I know her background. She is a psychologist with a specialist PhD in advanced conditioning. From the look of his records, she spent a really long time with him.

(pauses)

But what could that mean?

What could Doctor Saul have done to him?

What do they need conditioning for? I thought this was purely medical; I didn't know his mental capacity was being tested or influenced in any way.

I don't know. Maybe I don't really know what I'm talking about.I never was interested much in psychology. I loved the biology of how things worked, loved understanding the chemistry of our bodies and which chemicals did what – but I never cared about what was in a person's mind. That bordered too much on philosophy, and that wasn't for me – I deal with solid facts, and solid research.

But, right now, I'd love to know what's going on behind these eyes. This person – subject – their eyes, they just, they seem so...

(shrugs)

I waited for a reaction.

Waited and waited.

Two hours later, subject still hadn't moved. I took some of the subject's blood to see how it responded.

It read like human blood.

I placed a drop of infected blood on it, and before I got to the microscope, the infection had already engulfed the subject's blood and taken over, you can see that without needing to zoom in.

There is no immunity there.

Not that it's immunity I'm after, but it's a general expectation that...

This is not the right dose.

This is frustrating me. I thought I had it.

Maybe I just need to increase it.

Yeah, I'll increase it.

(computer makes sound)

(reads computer screen)

Great. So Doctor Emma Saul will be speaking to the subject again. Alone. Without me.

I objected to this, but no, they've messaged back and – well, they do not care. I said that if my tests are to continue, I am to know what all the variables are. This includes what they are doing to him with the psychologist. What it is they need to involve conditioning for.

They told me it's above my pay grade.

Maybe I can tell them I won't do the synthesis then. They can find someone else.

(pause)

No, I can't say that. I wouldn't.

I want to say it. Tell them they can find someone else.

But, I – I can't. I know what would happen to me if I did. I know where I would end up.

Then again, I don't exactly know what would happen, or where I'd end up – that's why I can't object to any of this.

I may be good, but there's nothing that special about what I do. There are plenty of other doctors like me. Plenty who could take my research, take my work, and reproduce it.

If it's not me, it's someone else.

So I will prepare for tomorrow.

I will increase the dosage of the mutation.

Hope that this works.

Hope that it satisfies the great, almighty prime minister. And just continue as I am.

I just...

I don't understand what we're doing to this man.

Sorry.

I don't understand what we're doing to this subject.

48 HOURS TO TRAP

Chapter Nineteen

Gus felt pathetic.

Worse than pathetic.

Abysmal. Humiliated. An incompetent fool.

He was a goddamn army hero, for Christ's sake. Not some idiot reliant on other people to survive. He'd never relied on another person for a day in his life, and he prided himself on it. Yet, there he was, his arm draped around an impartial Donny, who nonchalantly helped Gus slowly limp between the trees, dodging the bushes and sinking his single, leftover leg into the soft squelch of the watered soil beneath.

It wouldn't be as bad if Donny acknowledged it. Made a joke, like he often would. Something immensely ill-timed and poorly constructed, but a joke that made light of the situation nonetheless. But Donny just kept his arm firmly around Gus, keeping him balanced, ignoring any attempt at conversation.

Which, of course, Gus was partly grateful for; he was out of breath as it was, and conversation would prove irritating. It was just so unlike Donny to not be talking all the time. So much so, that when his awkward chatter ceased, it left a blank space hovering in the air around him. Like something needed to be filled that he wasn't filling, a void only his idle chatter would fill.

"You okay?" Gus asked, reluctantly attempting to drag words out of Donny, disguised as a check on Donny's welfare.

"Fine."

Donny was more than fine.

He had barely slowed for hours. He had all of Gus's weight rested upon him, supporting the guy's balance – and Gus wasn't a small guy – yet there was no sweat, no break in his strides, no quiver of his strength.

Donny had been unfit and unprepared. Now he didn't falter one bit. This was too unlike him.

A headrush burst upon Gus's mind. He'd been getting them more and more frequently in the last hour. Made sense, really; they must have been pumping him full of drugs at the compound after amputating his leg, and he knew he would be getting withdrawal symptoms at some point – but he had to keep going. He couldn't afford to pass out.

He was already enough of a burden on Sadie and Donny as it was.

Before, it had been the other way around. Donny was the burden on him. Gus would be driving toward London, mind focussed on his mission, trying to do all he could to ignore Donny's drivel.

"You know what I want," Donny had blurted out on such an occasion.

Gus had closed his eyes in that way you do when you're annoyed, fed up, wishing for everything to just go away. He rubbed his hand over his face and just concentrated on the road ahead.

"A sword," Donny declared. "No, not a sword. A hacksaw."

A hacksaw?

"What the –" Gus began, then interrupted himself. He

mustn't bite. He mustn't engage. Otherwise, that would open up pointless conversation.

Too late.

"Yeah, I mean, we all should have a weapon of choice in a zombie apocalypse, right?"

A zombie apocalypse? This guy lives in a bloody fantasy...

"I mean, on my computer game, it was either a sword, machete, or gun. But I always fancied a hacksaw."

Gus scoffed. The kid was comparing this to a computer game.

Gus had played *Call of Duty*. He'd also served in Iraq and Afghanistan. The experience was substantially, incontrovertibly, unequivocally different.

"But, see, a hacksaw – this is what I'm thinking – a hacksaw has different functions. So a gun is loud, that attracts a horde, that's the last resort, right? Well, a knife would also be good. You can get all stabby-stabby. But then what do you do when you need to detach their limb as it grabs onto you?"

Gus sighed. Was the kid still going?

"And you can't go through a limb in a clean swipe with a knife, and it has no give for sawing something off. So, a hacksaw can act as a stabby-stabby thing, right – and it can also detach limbs. You get my meaning?"

Gus shook his head. Get his meaning? There was nothing about Donny's meaning he got.

"What would be your weapon of choice?" Donny asked.

Gus didn't reply.

"I see you as, like, a curved blade kind of guy. What's those weapons that have a curved blade? Like a moon crescent shape. You know what I mean?"

"A scythe?"

Dammit, Gus scolded himself. *I replied.*

"Yes! That's it! Primarily used for gardening, of course, but also good in a fight." Donny beamed at Gus for finally engaging. "You know your weapons, my friend."

What a difference a few months would make.

Gus thought about that conversation, with his arm draped around his silent companion, as he watched the oblivious silence of Donny's face. Reacting to nothing. Not even Gus's stare, which he was sure Donny noticed.

What he'd give for another stupid conversation about now.

Chapter Twenty

Stealth. A skill normally attributed to being a result of other skills: acceleration, vigilance, cunning.

Nonsense.

Stealth wasn't the result – it was the cause. Everything about a good spy, a good attack, came down to stealth. Without it, there was no way Desert could have tracked those three strangers without being noticed. As it was, she barely rustled a leaf, barely made an audible breath. Her eyes were glued to them the whole time, as they remained completely and utterly oblivious.

Her home remained unnoticed. Covered by green. Undiscovered and unperturbed.

But these three... miscreants. They were strange. An odd combination, and by the state of them, strange that they would have lasted this long.

A little woman, more like a wildcat than a person, ran ahead; sometimes on her legs, sometimes on all fours. She sniffed the air. She peered into the distance. She was their watch, their protection; she formed the head of the triad, yet at the same time, had an odd dynamic. She would continually look back for the other's approval. She wasn't just checking if they were following, she was checking they were happy with her as a lookout. It was like she was part of a pack, and they were the ones she had to lead.

Though, once you looked at the other two, it became clear why she was the one chosen to protect, despite initially being such a surprising choice.

Firstly, the big guy had no leg. He looked like he was in charge from the way he carried himself, like he was the decision-maker – yet he was the most vulnerable of the lot of them. His arm was draped around a man who had one facial expression. As if his mouth and eyes had been stuck in some vacantly demented frown. Still, he loyally supported the other man, with a sturdiness his frame didn't justify – he just didn't look like he was meant to be at the guy's side. Like he didn't belong.

But then again, none of them looked like they belonged. Like they were just three idiots who drew the short straw.

So how had they survived?

She could ask such questions later. They were getting too close. Too close to discovering Desert's refuge. She'd spent too long protecting it; she wasn't about to let these people run into a concealed entrance by happy mistake.

She drew her gun.

She loved that gun.

Black. Semi-automatic. A handgun that wasn't small enough to be pathetic, but wasn't too large to fit snuggly in her hand.

What a difference almost a year had made to her.

She wasn't the woman she once was. The suit-wearing office-dweller, meeting everyone else's needs, sucking up to the boss, working desperately for a living, bending over, letting guys use her, lonely, bored, oh please can I help, please can I answer your email, Mr Squire, please can I ignore the fact that you're fucking everything behind your wife's back that moves, can I just pretend that you're fine even though you stare at my tits and make a pass at me every morning you walk in and ask if you have any messages you chauvinistic arsehole piece of shit.

When she'd recovered from the initial shock, she wasn't even that surprised Eugene had killed his wife.

In fact, being honest, she rued herself for not seeing it coming.

She was unrecognisable now. She was not the pathetic person she once was. She could shoot a gun with the precision of a superior predator on useless prey. Her delicate, long, blond hair was replaced with a lethal mohawk. Her snazzy suit gone in place of combat trousers, a belt of ammo, and a tight, black vest. Her face no longer wore the doormat sign or the eager-to-be-liked grimace of intimidation she'd attached to her visage each day; she wore a defiant snarl, a prowling glare, and a kick-arse attitude no fucker would mess with.

She'd left Lucy Sanders behind in that compound.

Safety off. She took aim. The three misfits came closer. Not of their own accord, but out of their dumb luck, dumb luck that was sure to get them killed.

Not that she needed the gun.

Her traps were impeccable. Whizzo had put them together and she'd laid them, concealing them around the perimeter, hidden by the green décor, the mountainous peaks, the glorious trees.

What a lovely forest it was.

She crouched, making her way further along her viewpoint, keeping them in her sight. Her tiptoes made a swift silence upon the absent rustles of the tedious leaves. She was sure it was spring. A comfortable sunniness hung overhead, and trees converged upon the soft soil in nature's effervescence.

They were too close.

Desert was sure they didn't deserve to die. These three hadn't the ability to harm anyone. She was sure.

Then again, a guy doesn't lose his leg for nothing. A person doesn't have a face of stone without experiences. And a girl doesn't become that animalistic without a cause.

No, she couldn't take chances. She'd proceed with caution.

They stumbled. The man with one leg putting too much weight on the guy keeping him upright.

The girl tried to help.

And they all stepped into the net, which trapped them, then lifted them into the sky, where they dangled helplessly.

Desert stepped out and aimed her gun.

"Who the fuck are you?" she demanded.

Chapter Twenty-One

They had been travelling for days. Gus was keen for them to keep moving, to put as much distance between them and the compound as they could, but he was struggling.

There were no vehicles, no houses, no resources, nothing they were coming across. Occasionally they came across green life bearing fruit and they had a few bites, but hunger was kicking in. Not to mention drug withdrawals. The dizziness he felt only highlighted precisely how much medication they must have been using to numb the pain of his absent leg, to ensure he didn't kick up a fuss about it – but his withdrawals had gone beyond a head rush now. The world was turning to blurs; every few seconds a new migraine, the chirps of the birds a distant haze. The world was becoming more disconnected from him by the hour. He wasn't sure how much longer he could go.

But Donny – he hadn't moaned once. The amount of weight Gus was putting on him seemed to make no difference. He repeatedly asked whether Donny needed a break, suggesting intermittent rest. Donny didn't need it. He would reply every time with the same robotic, "I do not need to rest."

The guy was freaking him out.

But that could have just been his perception of it. He was aware enough to know he wasn't very aware. The world around him was distorted, hopelessly unclear.

He wondered if he was going to survive.

Sadie rushed ahead, turning back, looking to Gus. What did she want, approval? Confirmation? Affirmation? What?

Whatever it was, Gus couldn't give it to her.

She'd done amazingly so far, and he was so grateful to her, but he was being honest with himself – they were fucked. The middle of a forest, miles and miles of nothing. It was like the world had gone even further to shit since they'd been captured.

Where were the survivors?

Gus knew they were sparse, but where were they? Surely being surrounded by trees would be the best camouflage. A rural place, away from the cities, away from prying eyes. If Gus was still with his family, that's where he'd have taken them.

His family. Janet. Laney.

No matter how delirious he got, their faces were always imprinted on the forefront of his mind.

He fell. Out of nowhere. Collapsed.

Donny tried to support him. Tried to catch him.

Gus was on his knees.

He heard a gun click.

Way off. Far away. Somewhere. It clicked.

He looked to Sadie. She didn't have a gun. She didn't even know how to work a gun. She was better than a gun.

Donny. Did he know how to work a gun?

He looked up, cast his eyes up and down his friend. Nothing registered. What was he even looking for?

A click.

A gun.

That's it.

He looked to Donny's hand. There were four of them, all skewed, dancing around him, taunting him. No gun.

He was sure he heard a click.

"Donny... Sadie..."

Sadie rushed over.

"I heard..."

Someone was there. He was sure of it.

Was he sure of it?

He didn't really know what was going on.

What had he heard?

There was a...

What was going on?

He tried to stand. Donny tried to support him. Sadie tried to support him. They failed. He stumbled. He took them with them.

His foot stepped on the net.

He was in the air before he knew it.

Was he flying?

No, he was hovering. He reached his arm out, felt for nearby. Donny was there. He could see him. His face. So stern. Sadie was there. She was screaming, she hated it.

"Sadie," Gus prompted, willing her to shush, which she did.

He tried to kick. He couldn't. He'd forgotten. He looked up and his stump was thrashing about.

His hands grabbed the net.

How did they end up there?

A prompt flashback. A few hours ago. Or was it days? Donny. He said he knew where they were going. He said he knew where it was. Where what was?

Where had Donny taken them?

Before Gus could entertain the thought anymore, it faded from his mind like steam into air.

He closed his eyes for longer than he expected. Closed them. Opened them.

A gun was pointing at them from below.

"Who the fuck are you?" demanded the person behind it.

Chapter Twenty-Two

She wasn't the kind of woman who was like fire – Desert was fire.

And not just your flickering candle waving easily in the wind, either.

She was raging flames, she was burning amber, she was fire that spread and engulfed everything within its path. Her anger would lash out at you, licking your feet with the scorching heat of wrathful flames. Her passion would entice you into its growing torch as its smoke paraded into the sky. And her tenacity; oh, her tenacity. It was the lava the flames created. Pure, boastful, crackling, whipping, fiery lava that left ashes in its wake.

"I asked you a question," she said, exuding dominance, showing nothing but her boss-like attitude you either came to respect or fear.

The girl – (*woman?*) – hissed at her. Reached its hand through the net, too far into the sky to be able to reach but reaching nonetheless.

Desert sighed.

"I am one itchy trigger finger away from shooting the shit

out of you unless you answer my question," Desert continued, aiming her semi-automatic.

"It's okay," the one-legged man said to the girl. "She's just being cautious, it's okay."

"Talk to me, or I'll shoot her in the face."

"How about you just cool it, yeah?" the man blurted out. "Just cool it."

Desert looked to the other man, his stoic expression unfaltering.

"What's with him?" Desert demanded.

"He – we – we've been through a lot, okay. It's – could you just let us down from this?"

"I'm thinking not."

Gus's hand moved.

"Keep your hand in the air!" Desert shouted. "So much as scrape a finger on a pistol and I won't be taking any chances."

"Fine, fine – what d'you want to know?"

"Who are you?"

"My name is Gus Harvey, this is Sadie, and this is Donny Jevon."

"Okay, Gus. How d'you lot know each other?"

"It's... It's kind of a long story."

"Yeah, well, you better tell it. 'Cause this whole picture, the three of you together, it – it just don't fit. And when something don't fit..."

"All right, all right."

Desert waited.

Gus rubbed his head, closed his eyes, kept them closed a prolonged moment, opened them, shut them again.

"Well?"

"Just – just give me a minute. I think I'm going to pass out."

"Why?"

"You see this?" Gus indicated his leg. "Yeah? You see this? This is a recent thing, lady. This got done to me, and I've not had any of the shit they pumped into me, and without the shit they pumped into me, I'm getting kinda woozy, so if you'd just–"

"Who's they?"

"What?"

"You keep saying they. Who is they? Who did this to you?"

Gus sighed.

"You wouldn't believe me."

"Pretty sure I would."

"You heard of a dickhead named Eugene Squire?"

Desert's finger hovering over the trigger lapsed its concentration for a heartbeat. A familiar rage grew inside of her, starting with the acidity of her stomach, lifting through her thrashing heart, and ending in her tightened throat. She couldn't breathe. Why couldn't she breathe?

That name.

That damn name.

"Yeah. Yeah, I heard of him."

"He did this to me. Well – not himself directly."

"I don't believe you."

"Thought you might not."

"What else did he do?"

"We've been trapped in his compound, he's – just look at the state of us."

Desert looked at the other two. Being closer to the girl's face, finally having a look at it, revealed bruises that only came from torture. Scabs, wounds, tears. And worse; scars the girl probably hadn't even made sense of yet appeared in her eyes. A look so familiar.

The other man's face wasn't so readable. His eyes gave nothing away. His expression was deadened. He just looked back at her with a severe impartiality. A neglectful absence of caring.

Him, she wasn't so sure about.

"And who are you?" the man called Gus asked.

She wondered whether she should trust them.

Unfortunately, people to trust didn't come along too often these days.

"My name is Desert," she declared.

Then she aimed her gun at the girl's head.

Chapter Twenty-Three

"Desert? I assume that's a code name?"

Just keep her talking.

That's all Gus could think to do.

Keep her talking.

This was about survival. Short-term living. Staying alive. Somehow finding a way to make it through the next few hours. Then the next few hours would come after that, and the next after that, and the next after that. Eventually, hours could turn into days, maybe even weeks, months, years.

But for now, the one who called herself Desert was aiming her gun at Sadie's head, and Gus didn't like it.

"It's fine," he said. "You don't have to tell me your real name. Just – just..."

Just what, Gus?

He had no idea what to say. How could he reason with her? If it were he in her predicament, would he take any chances? Or would he shoot the three weirdos who'd stumbled across his patch?

His eyes closed.

For too long.

He could feel himself slipping away. He had a few fingers keeping a very loose grip on consciousness, and he was slipping, sliding off, with no one to catch him.

He had to keep her talking. Had to do something.

“Please, Eugene Squire almost killed us. Don’t be the same as him.”

Desert’s arm relaxed.

That did it. Boy, that did it. Something on her face changed, something softened, if only momentarily. Her steely neutrality shifted, and Gus saw what trigger lay beneath.

“I am nothing like Eugene Squire,” Desert spat. “And don’t you dare ever say that again.”

“If Eugene Squire is your enemy, then our enemy makes us a friend.”

Desert didn’t respond.

“Please, I...” He almost went again. Drooped. Faded in and out. Brought himself around. “I... I have no idea what I was saying.”

“Why should I trust you?”

“What?”

“Eugene Squire would want me dead. This is exactly the kind of thing–”

“Look at my leg!” Gus cried. “Seriously, look at my fucking leg! Look at what he did to my leg! It’s gone ’cause of him, why would I–”

A pain shot in the base of his stump.

He hadn’t felt pain there before. It was as if all the medication he’d been given at the compound was designed to numb it, and whilst his dizziness was the first price to pay, it was just the start.

Burning raced around the circumference of his knee. Then a stabbing sensation, like someone had sunk a knife in, then another, until his leg was full of their sharp edges, all sticking out of him, like a sadistic acupuncturist who used blades instead of needles. It hurt to holy hell.

Gus screamed out.

"Shut up, you'll attract a horde."

He bit his lip. Useless. He opened his mouth, cried out again. Moaned into the rope.

"Listen," Gus said. "You are either going to have to shoot me or let me down, 'cause this–"

It hit him in another wave, surging all through his body this time; he could feel it pulsating, throbbing through him to the rhythm of his pulse.

His arms flung out to the side, clutching the rope, squeezing it tightly, tightly, tighter, biting it, keeping himself from screaming out.

He closed his eyes. Opened them. Everything was gone. A distant distortion. Impressions of shapes were there in blurs. Someone was speaking but it was as if they were underwater.

He screamed again.

Then he felt himself falling. He didn't know how. Hell, he didn't even know if it was real. It was like he was collapsing downwards through the sky.

Janet.

Laney.

I see you.

That wasn't them. He knew it.

There was no afterlife.

But he saw them. Waving to him. Their faces turning to blood.

He was being carried. There were people around him. He felt them as he reached his arms out and grabbed them. He was then restrained.

Where was he again?

Janet. So far. In touching distance, yet however much he

reached out for her, he could never brush his fingers down her soft cheek.

Laney was playing. She turned and said hello. Or did she? Gus didn't hear her.

They disappeared.

They weren't there. He knew they weren't there.

He had no idea where he was anymore.

He didn't even care.

And, on that final thought, his delirium ended and he fell completely unconscious.

Chapter Twenty-Four

The light overhead wasn't buzzing. His legs weren't fixed to a bed. An uncaring doctor wasn't spoon-feeding him lumps.

This was the first time Gus had woken up from falling unconscious without laying in torment. It was a sealed room without windows, leading Gus to the logical conclusion that he was underground. If they had encroached on this woman's home without noticing it, it must be.

He flexed his hands, looking at them. Wiggled his leg, wiggled his stump. How strange it was to wake up free from restrictions. It was like he was waking up in a bed for the first time ever.

"Good morning."

Gus jumped, turned his head to see the woman sat beside him.

"We have a lot to talk about," she stated.

"Where's Sadie?" Gus demanded, gripping the side of the bed. "Where's Donny?"

He scanned the room for a weapon.

"Relax, relax," she urged him. "They are being fed. In fact, they've been fed three times. You know, tea, breakfast, and lunch."

"That how long I've been out?"

"Yep."

"I want to see them. I want to see they are okay."

"Please, I'm not going to hurt you. If I was going to hurt you, why would I have wasted medical supplies on you?"

Gus looked around him. He was attached to a drip. The pain in his right thigh had gone, presumably from another dose of the right medication. What's more, there was a flower in a vase in the corner of the room, and the pillow beneath him smelt like lavender.

He looked the woman over. Strange hair, but he liked it. It was individual. She was sat back, so relaxed, with a posture that didn't say she didn't care, yet still said she was chilled; her hand draped over the back of her chair and her foot resting on the knee of her other leg.

"What did you say your name is again?" Gus asked.

"Desert."

"That's not a name."

Desert sighed.

"It is. Though I've had it for less than a year. I felt like I needed a change of name."

"What's your real name? Why are you pretending to–"

"Gus, Gus, please, relax. You're fine, but stressing out ain't going to do much for your body; you need rest."

"I want to know–"

"And I'm here to tell you. I'm here to tell you everything. Just relax."

Gus went to retaliate, then decided against it. She was probably right. It had been a hard few days. Hell, it had been a hard few months. Years, even. And this was the softest mattress he'd ever laid on. He should probably take advantage.

Desert sat forward, leaning toward him with her hands clasped together.

"My name used to be Lucy Sanders."

"Lucy Sanders..."

"I used to work for Eugene Squire. I was a receptionist."

"I couldn't see you as a receptionist."

"Yeah, I've changed a fair bit." She chuckled. "But I was, suit and everything. Walked around with doormat written on my forehead. Then I found out what they were trying to do."

She smiled a knowing smile that drew him in.

"I was there, Gus. At the beginning. I was there, I saw it."

"What? You mean, you know how this all started?"

She nodded two large triumphant nods.

"Parliament was wiped out by the infected. I was the one who had to deliver the message to Eugene Squire, not just that they had died, but that he was next in line to be prime minister. He was about thirtieth in line, but that's what it had come to. I was stupid not to realise – Eugene had engineered it all."

"How?"

"General Boris Hayes. He'd released the strain when Parliament was in session and Eugene was on annual leave with his wife."

"He has a wife?"

"Had a wife. He killed her in front of me."

"Jesus..."

Desert took in a big, deep breath, then let it out. Something told Gus she wasn't used to telling this story.

"So why did he do it?" Gus asked.

"He didn't mean to create an infection, not at first. They spoke as they... Well, they tried to kill me. From what I gathered, they were trying to create something else, and the infection was just the catalyst. Something that had an ability to run faster, be stronger, but... When he accidentally engineered a virus, he used it to put himself in power, and give him an advantage over other countries."

"Other countries?"

"That bombing on London... I don't know yet, I'm basing this on assumptions. But I don't think it was as simple as we think."

"I was there. I was there when it was bombed. London was a mess."

"It wasn't bombed by us. We don't know much, but we know that for sure."

Gus tried to take this all in, but only fell further into a migraine. He looked around himself.

"So what is this place?"

"An underground bunker used by the AGA. Well, it used to be."

"The AGA?"

"The Anti-Government Alliance. The last line of defence against Eugene Squire. Except..."

"Except what?"

"I think you'd better take a look."

Desert took a pair of crutches from behind her and offered them to him.

Chapter Twenty-Five

Gus marvelled at the vastness of the place. There was a large, open area that could be filled with tanks, armies, weapons, everything. Except it was empty.

It was a hollow excitement; such optimism, yet such absence.

This was such a great base, such a great resource – so where was this AGA? Why weren't they using it?

"So. this AGA," Gus said. "You it?"

Desert grinned. "That would be disappointing, wouldn't it? Our only remaining defence, and it was just me?"

Gus watched her. She was so confident, so supreme, yet, at the same time, alluring. There was something about her that made you want to follow her.

"Let me introduce you to my crew."

Desert opened a door and they entered a canteen. The tables were mostly empty, and there was nobody serving any food – but the central table was full.

Sadie and Donny sat on one side of the table. Upon seeing Gus, Sadie leapt to her feet, ran toward him and almost knocked him over with her embrace, squeezing him tight.

"Hey," Gus managed.

Gus looked to Donny. They exchanged a look. Donny nodded. Gus returned the mild sentiment.

"Here's my crew." Desert pointed out the two people sat opposite Sadie and Donny. "This is Whizzo."

A young lad stopped hoovering down his food long enough to nod at Gus and give him a cheeky smile. The kid held Gus's focus – he looked far too young to be part of a resistance.

"You old enough to be in this AGA?"

"I'm seventeen," Whizzo pointed out. "And you find me somebody who can do the shit I can do and I'll happily go to bed."

"Whizzo," Desert said, "is a technical whiz kid – hence the code name. Any contraption, electrical device, engineering, anything – he can sort it. He is right, the shit he can do is amazing."

"You know," Whizzo said, finishing his last few mouthfuls of rice, "I could do something for that, if you want."

"For what?"

"That stump you got there. The missing leg. I'm sure I could fix something up."

Gus went to object, claim defensively he didn't need the kid's help, then wondered why he was doing that. He'd only been walking around with one leg for a few days and it was already proving tricky enough.

Still, Gus wasn't one for handouts.

"I'll be fine," he concluded.

"And this is Prospero."

The older fella next to Whizzo nodded. He had a bushy moustache beneath his lip, was well-built, yet looked considerably older than the other two.

"Prospero used to be in Hayes' army."

"Oh yeah?"

"Not just that," Prospero declared, his voice suiting his army persona. "I was sergeant in the navy, commander in Iraq, and then – well, you know who I served then."

"I get it," Gus said. "I served too."

He turned to Desert, rotating on his crutches with little skill – they were taking some getting used to. And, despite having only just gotten up, he was feeling awfully tired.

"If this AGA is the last defence, then where is it?" Gus asked. "I mean, don't get me wrong, I'm grateful for you not shooting us and all that – but where is it?"

Desert sighed. She exchanged eye contact with her crew. Whizzo shrugged, as if to say, *you may as well tell him.* Prospero gave her a subtle nod of approval.

"A few months ago," Desert explained, "we were in a fight. A big one. Hayes' army was too much. Most of us got killed. The rest of us... got separated. We ended up here."

"And the rest?"

Desert shrugged. "We've been trying to track them, but no luck."

"So you have no idea where they are?"

"Not exactly."

"There's a base," Prospero took over. "About twenty, thirty miles from here. It's our emergency base, where we're meant to meet should anything go wrong."

"So why haven't you gone there?" Gus enquired.

Whizzo laughed, then choked on the last bite of his food. "You been outside lately?"

"Yeah. I have."

"Then you know it's swarming with those things."

"But now you're here," Desert said. "We have numbers. We have another ex-serviceman. Your friends seem to be useful. Maybe you could help us?"

"Help you?"

"It's our only shot."

Gus bowed his head. Hesitated. Looked at his leg. Looked at his crutches.

"I don't know," he spoke, softly and quietly. "I'm not really much of a help nowadays. More of a burden."

"Like I said," Whizzo interrupted, "I could sort something out for–"

"It don't matter!" Gus snapped. "I..."

He could feel tiredness taking over. He was getting lethargic. Quick to bite. He needed rest.

"If you don't mind, I'd appreciate you directing me back to that bed. I'm not feeling too great."

Desert exchanged a solemn look with the others, then resigned herself to agreement.

"Fine. This way."

Gus followed her.

He knew she wanted better news. He knew she probably deserved it. Anyone standing up to Eugene Squire was a friend to him. But he felt useless. Worse than useless. Inept. He wouldn't just be unable to contribute to their operation; he'd hinder it. They'd have to slow down for him. They'd have to go back and protect him. What could he do with one leg against a horde?

No. It was sad to admit it, but he had to admit it.

His life doing the impossible was over now. It was time to retire.

The Journal of Doctor Janine Stanton

Day 2

Transcript from webcam journal by Janine Stanton, second entry

Transcript from webcam journal by Janine Stanton, second entry

I HAD LITTLE SLEEP LAST NIGHT. I DON'T KNOW. I GUESS THIS is getting to me. It's tough. I don't know what I'm doing. Well, I do, it's just – I don't know why I'm doing it. And I don't know what Eugene is going to do with it when it's done.

I gave him – the subject, I mean – I gave the *subject* a second dose:

35% BLOOD OF MUTATION
- 5% blood of infected
- 15% blood of infected
- 18% ketorolac
- 15% cortisone
- 12% water

. . .

As you can see, I've depleted the content of water significantly. More than half, in fact. And I have increased the blood of mutation by seven percent, but the blood of infected only by two – I am worried that, by giving him blood of infected, it will take over. I am increasing that one warily.

Yet, he's not becoming infected. At least not visibly, anyway.

The rest is working in that respect. But, it just doesn't – doesn't do what Eugene wants.

I made such promises. What if I can't do it?

Then again – what if I do?

(pause)

I did the check-up on him three hours after administering the dose. Honestly, infected blood acts within a minute, but I left it a length of time, as his own blood may have diluted it, the mutation blood may have diluted it, the painkillers and steroids may have...

Eyeballs were the same. No excessive dilation. Breathing pattern remained. Heartbeat regular. Well, existent – not like the infected.

But, he's not becoming the infected, is he?

What is he becoming?

Eugene, if you find this, then...

Then what?

What are you–

(cries)

Oh, heck. Stop it, Janine. Get over yourself. This is your job.

Is it?

My job?

I mean, don't people get paid for their – it's just, I'm here because I'm required, I'm fed, but, I don't know.

Should this be my duty?

But my duty for what! Oh, I'm fed up with just going off on one. I should be focussed on my work, should stop thinking about what I'm doing, why I'm doing it – I'm doing it for the government, so surely, surely, there's got to be good reason?

But if there's good reason, why do I feel like I'm here against my will?

(pause)

Subject isn't reacting. But he is still. So, so still. Like, his finger occasionally twitches, but that's it. His eyes focus on a point in the room. Beside that, sometimes, you wouldn't even know he's breathing, except for the occasional cough, and even then, I have to look twice to check I did actually hear a cough.

What did Doctor Emma Saul do to him?

I'd love to read her notes. I'm told they are classified.

Classified.

(shakes head)

But why would they have classified actions of a conditioning expert, if they weren't conditioning him to – I don't know. What? Be more placid? Be unreactive, passive, uncaring? He doesn't even acknowledge my existence. What could they possibly have done?

I bet Pavlov and his dogs would kick themselves if they knew his work was being used for something like this.

But something like what?

Urgh, stop it.

(long pause)

I slept at my desk last night. He was awake when I fell asleep, I remember that, and then, when I woke up – he was still awake. But he wasn't even watching me. I just couldn't believe I fell asleep in the room, I – he didn't even seem to have noticed.

Does he even sleep?

(sighs)

I just want to go home. I want to get this over with.

This afternoon I am preparing the dose for tomorrow, and, I

– I'm going to take a risk. Up the blood of the infected. See if that does anything. If it takes over, then, well, at least I know he won't end up as they want him to. He'll be saved from that.

We'll all be saved from that.

32 HOURS TO TRAP

Chapter Twenty-Seven

Gus was awoken by giggling. Childish, infantile giggling. He instantly felt irritable. Perturbed. Annoyed. What was going on? Who was disturbing his sleep? Didn't anyone tell them to let sleeping bastards lie?

"What is going on?" Gus demanded, his voice gruff.

The giggling continued.

"What is it?"

Gus leant up, and all around him, they stood. Sadie, Donny, Whizzo, Prospero, and Desert. They were all in fits of excitable chuckles; except Donny, who stood their impartially numb, as seemed to be his regular stance.

"What do you want!" Gus persisted. "Why the hell are you wrecking my sleep?"

They looked to each other. Exchanged smiles.

What the hell were they smiling about?

"He's not even noticed," Desert pointed out, like they were all part of some secret society that Gus wasn't privy to. "I can't believe he's not even noticed. How does he not feel that?"

"Not feel what? What the hell have you done!"

Whizzo playfully raised his hand with a cheeky grin.

"I'll have to take credit for it," Whizzo said, then raised his hands to the side, as if to say, *couldn't help it.* "Why don't you check it out?"

Gus leant up. Now he was getting pissed.

"Check what out? Why are you in here? What are you on about?"

"I said I'd make you one," Whizzo said, pointing downwards.

Gus leant up and looked down.

Oh, Jesus.

He didn't know what to say. What to think.

Anger for the pertinence? Annoyance for the audacity? Or sheer appreciation for the effort?

He turned and placed his new prosthetic leg on the ground. It wasn't what he expected a prosthetic leg to look like. In fact, it looked nothing like a leg. It was a curved piece of metal upon a spring, somehow stuck to him.

He tugged on it.

"How do you get it off?" Gus barked.

"You'd have to detach it from the bone," Whizzo replied.

"You what!"

"Gus," Desert interjected, "before you jump down his throat for trying to help you, why don't you check it out, yeah? Then, if you're pissed, you can say."

Gus shook his head. He was fuming. A boiling kettle ready to overflow.

He stood, ready to go for them – then paused.

He balanced. Easily. More easily than he'd expected.

The spring gave a nice response to the floor, hard enough so as not to give way, but soft enough to react to his movement.

Gus looked to the others. He did not know what to think. His anger was quickly fading, but he wanted to hold onto it, remain stubborn in his ways.

Yet, at the same time, he was astonished. This could change

everything.

"It has six strong spring clamps with metal springs," Whizzo explained, "with titanium metal beneath a coating of stainless steel and chromium, to unsure it doesn't rust. The thing is practically faultless."

"Why don't you try it out?" Desert prompted.

Gus took a few steps. He had a slight limp, but it worked. He could walk again. On his own accord.

"I didn't mean in here," Desert said. "I meant out there."

The open room. With the vast amount of space.

But what if he fell? What if he landed flat on his arse and looked like a complete fool?

"It'll be difficult at first," Whizzo pointed out. "But once you've got your handle on it, you'll barely even notice."

"Honestly, he's been working on it all night. Just go have a run. We won't laugh."

With a glance of trepidation their way, he edged toward the door. He looked back at Sadie, who smiled excitedly.

He left the confines of the bedroom and entered the open space. Stood, viewing the vast emptiness he had to run into. He felt nervous. Why? It wasn't like this was the first time he'd ever walked. Except, in a way, it was; it was like he was exploring the world all over again.

He started out in a light jog. He stumbled to the side a little but didn't break stride. He kept going. Surging on. Powering forward.

He sped up. A run. A gentle run, but he was going faster. And he was doing it without a care in the world.

He made the decision to see how fast he could go. He found a whole new dose of confidence, he felt ready, he was willing to see how far he could stretch this leg.

He sprinted. As fast as he could.

If anything, he went faster than when he had two good legs. The springs propelled him forward. The metal didn't shake, quiver, or anything. It remained sturdy, like it was part of him, like it always had been.

He screamed joyous screams. Lifted his arms out and felt the wind rush through his fingers. Felt his breathing quicken pace, felt his heart race, felt everything in his body burst to keep up with him.

He was soaring. Like the first time he'd ever run, but better.

He turned full circle and ran back to where everyone was waiting. Out of breath, he stopped, put his hands on his knees, panted, let his body catch up, enjoyed the familiar aching, relished the stitch in his side.

"So," Desert said, "what do you think?"

Gus smiled. Beamed. Couldn't help it. The smile just plastered itself across his face and stayed there as if glued to him.

He stepped forward, took Whizzo's hand, and shook it, shook it hard, vigorously, with enough passion and enthusiasm to convey his appreciation.

"Thank you," asserted Gus. "Thank you so much."

"My pleasure," Whizzo replied.

"So what do you reckon, then?" Desert asked.

"What do you mean?"

"I mean, what do you think about helping us? About searching out the rest of the AGA?"

"I think..."

Gus looked down to his leg.

His leg.

His metal, springy, perfect, amazing leg.

He looked to Sadie. Eager.

"Of course," Gus said. "Of course, I'll help you. I mean, *we* will help you."

They smiled at each other, then Gus returned his gaze to his leg, astonished, marvelling.

The whole time, Donny stood there. Saying nothing but thinking everything.

Chapter Twenty-Eight

The night sky lit up with the peaceful tranquillity of dozens of stars. Lights from destruction far, far away. A thing of beauty, yet a thing of death.

Eugene wondered how long it would be until their star exploded.

His hands traced the outline of the barrier surrounding his porch. His flat was high up and, despite being quite afraid of heights, he enjoyed it; it meant he could condescend to all the tiny people on the street below. He'd spent many nights nursing a whiskey as he watched idiots wander about their pointless lives. Fools stumbling home drunk, soon-to-be-broken-hearted-lovers wrapped up in their own hysteria, the pointless lives of the homeless searching out a shop porch. Now, there was only the aimlessly wandering infected – and they were just as pathetic. Every now and then their heads would jerk, as if sensing food, possibly via a whiff on the air or the scuttle of a rat – usually, it would turn out to be nothing, and they would continue staggering down the street. Funny, really, how they were so slow and sluggish, but once the prospect of food announced itself their speed was unmatchable, and their ferocity unleashed.

Just like my ex-wife.

He laughed to himself. An unspoken joke with his thoughts.

Behind him, Hayes was still in the flat, pouring himself a fifty-year-old Balvenie Single Malt Scotch Whiskey. The flat itself was where he entertained his extra-marital affairs, its cost going down as an expense, of course. He missed the doorman who would greet him in the foyer, who would allow his guests up with such subtlety no one could rival. The walls were pristine, absent of any mark or dust; just pure, solid, impenetrable white.

The foyer was a wreck now, and the doorman was part of the undead, but what you going to do? Life goes on.

Hayes walked onto the porch, handing Eugene a tumbler of the exquisite whiskey, and joined in looking at the wretches below.

"Pitiful," Hayes observed. "Aren't they?"

Hayes could have been referring to many people: Gus Harvey, Gus Harvey's ratty friend, the AGA – but Eugene assumed Hayes was referring to the infected below.

Either way, the guy was correct.

"Yes," Eugene agreed, sipping his glass and relishing the beautiful sting of the first intake of scotch. "They are."

A moment of silence spoke of their mutual disdain for the beings they had created.

"Any word?" Eugene asked.

"Yep."

"And?"

"All affirmative. We are on track."

"Good. And the AGA?"

Hayes smiled cockily at Eugene.

"What do you take me for?" he asked.

Eugene grinned. Hayes was efficient, he had to give him that.

"So the trap..."

"Is on track. We will meet them, and we will take them out in a quick sweep."

"Good." Eugene leant against the wooden beam, exchanging glances between the dead below and the stars above. "I don't see them as a threat."

"But you just like to make sure."

"I'm like that. Like to keep things tidy."

"Say no more. It's done."

Eugene considered his next statement. He'd given it great thought, contemplating it every chance he got, and his decision had been made.

"I want to be there," he declared. "When it happens, I want to be there."

"Really?"

"Yes, really."

"Don't think it's a bit risky?"

"Think I can't handle it?"

Hayes paused. Considered his words.

"It's just a difficult situation, exposing you like that," Hayes stated. "You're the prime minister. You're in charge. If you get hurt–"

"I thought it was going to be a quick sweep, General."

"It is. But if you aren't protected in the initial attack–"

"Then you'll just have to make sure I am."

Hayes shrugged.

"Okay. We can do it. I'll put someone on you, make sure you're safe. You're the boss."

"Yes, I am."

Eugene sighed. Looked at his whiskey. Twirled his glass, watched the waves crash against the rim.

"I just don't want to work for all this," Eugene said, "and not be there to see it all come together."

"I understand."

"It's been such a bother, such a difficulty to make this all happen. Now it's going to happen, we're going to see it, actually see what we intended to create – I don't want to be sat at home waiting to hear all about it. I want to be there, to witness it. Once it happens, the AGA won't stand a chance anyway."

"They are pathetic. Depleted numbers. It's all precautionary."

Eugene put his hand on Hayes' shoulder.

"I place my trust in you, good sir."

"I won't let you down."

Eugene nodded.

No. He wouldn't.

Chapter Twenty-Nine

Lucy Sanders was dead.

That's all there was to it.

That pathetic morsel no longer meant anything to Desert. She wasn't some bitch to the office boss, some slut to the men who said a nice few words to get the most insecure woman in the bar into bed. Lucy Sanders had been more than the slave to the grind; she'd been the obedient, conforming, vagabond to the grind.

Now, she was the grind. She was the temptress who lured others into the fight against the life she once was.

Emotions didn't matter. They were there to be controlled, not unleashed. Everything she'd learnt up until now told her that she had to be ruthless, had to quell the useless instincts she'd had before.

Before the infection, she'd been a person who wore the nice clothes to work, did as she was told, waited and waited for that pay check to arrive at the end of the month and relished the week that it would last.

Now there was no pay check. There was survival.

And she was good at it.

After travelling for hours with no break, she appreciated Gus's suggestion to stop – but they'd stopped for too long now. They needed to get going. So, she readied herself. Prepared herself to continue.

The lake they'd found to rest beside flowed with steady waves, calmly thrashing its water against the bank. She dipped her bottle in, scooped up some water, lifted that bottle to her lips and relished the release from dehydration.

Funny, Lucy Sanders had never thought about how grateful she was for water. For the necessities of life she took for granted. For the pathetic existence that ruled her monotonous activities.

Desert was grateful. Every damn day.

Right. Enough rest. Desert concluded it was time to go, and approached Gus to voice this; but, as she approached, she couldn't help but watch.

Gus was sat next to Sadie who, despite her obvious limits in vocabulary, was listening intently to everything he said.

"The infected," Gus said, "the ones with the pale faces – can you tell the difference between them and us?"

Sadie eagerly nodded.

"So, the infected – what are they like?"

"Uh..." She considered this. "Fast. Bad. Uh... Dead."

"How can you tell they are dead?"

"Uh..." She indicated her face, then pulled a disgusting face.

Desert couldn't help but chuckle.

"Yes – they have disgusting faces," Gus confirmed, also smiling to himself. "And people who aren't infected – what do they look like?"

"Uh..." She thought intently. "Face... Nice. Alive."

"Yes, exactly. Now, here is the question – do we kill the infected" – he lifted his left hand out – "or do we kill the living?" He lifted his right hand out.

Sadie thought about this, then slapped Gus's left hand.

"Yes, excellent!"

Sadie smiled proudly to herself.

Gus held out his right hand, the one indicating the living.

"And the living – do we ever kill them?"

"Uh..."

"Think about it, Sadie. Is there ever a time we kill them?"

"Uh... Yeah?"

"Yeah. There is. Is it when you feel like it? Is it when you want them to go away?"

Sadie thought about this, then shook her head.

"Or – is it when you are in danger? When they are threatening your life, or one of your friend's lives?"

"Uh... Yeah."

"Excellent," Gus declared. "Good, Sadie. Well done."

Sadie beamed at Gus; she couldn't look prouder.

"Hey, Gus," Desert interrupted.

"What's up?"

"Reckon it's time to go?"

Gus shrugged. "Good a time as any."

They set off, walking back through the endless forest that consumed their surroundings. Desert was pretty sure they were in the middle of the Lake District – but she hadn't come across any signs, or any of the wooden posts that would have indicated a walking route one may have taken on a casual Saturday afternoon before the outbreak.

It didn't really matter. It wasn't like they needed to know the name of the forest. They just needed to go in the correct direction. Before the government's attack had left the AGA in scarce numbers, they'd had instructions on how to get there; head south east for forty to fifty miles. Expect radio transmission as you get closer.

But what if this place was no longer there? What if they didn't receive any transmission? What if–

No.

Lucy Sanders lived her life with what ifs.

Desert didn't.

Whizzo went to trip. Donny caught him, saving the young lad from an embarrassing slip into the water. An instinctive gesture of good will.

These were good people.

Gus's fatherly instinct toward Sadie, her undying loyalty, Donny's eagerness to avoid Whizzo getting hurt.

This all came from how much they cared about each other. From the strong hold their friendship had.

Strange, really. How such a thing can occur once the world had pretty much ended.

Maybe emotions weren't such a bad thing after all.

Chapter Thirty

He remembered.

Donny remembered.

He remembered who Gus was. Gus was the ex-soldier who abused him the whole way to London, who insinuated he was useless, who belittled him for no reason other than for being a no-good loser, hellbent on drinking himself to death over the demise of his family.

But there was something else.

More to Gus.

There were more memories. They just felt... concealed. Like they were on a shelf too high for him to reach, or were floating away from him on the waves of the shore and no matter how much he stretched his arm out, he couldn't reach them.

But there were feelings.

Again, feelings he didn't have. Or didn't recognise.

No, he had them, he was sure of it. He just didn't realise what they were.

Gus's leg. How did he end up with one leg? What happened? It seemed important, somehow. Like it was something Donny should know. Yet, the more he thought about it, the more he couldn't recall.

Donny had something to do with that leg being lost.

He knew he didn't do it. He knew that for sure. It didn't feel right. Gus did it to himself; that's what his instinct told him. That's what he was sure of. But why, and how? Such discoveries eluded him.

Still, Gus seemed happier with this new leg than he did with his old. He was gazing at it like a child with a new toy, marvelling at its innovation. Other people asked how he was getting on, his smile shone at them, saying stuff like, "I can't believe it," and "I'm so grateful," and "It's amazing."

Donny hung back. He felt a strange sense of responsibility to avoid being part of any social interaction, to avoid engaging in conversation about the AGA.

He glanced over his shoulder. All he saw was trees, but in his mind, he could still see the concealment of the AGA's barren underground headquarters. There was something about their expedition to find the rest of the AGA he knew. Something he was aware of, yet not aware of. Something he was sure of but had no way of knowing.

There is no AGA.

That was it. They didn't exist. He knew this – somehow, he absolutely knew their journey to the rest of the AGA was futile.

Again, he didn't know how he knew it. But, same as he knew he had ten fingers and ten toes, same as he knew his name was Donny, and same as he knew that he had to follow them and not let them out of his sight, he knew – there was no AGA.

The people they were looking for.

Their friends.

Useless.

Donny considered telling them. Rushing up to Desert and letting her know that this trip was pointless. That this search would lead nowhere.

But that wasn't what he was supposed to do.

He shook his head, attempting to snap himself out of it, out of this funk, out of this deep despondency that perplexed his mind.

Why was he so damn miserable?

He thought as far back as he could. He remembered Gus being an arsehole. As usual. A regular arsehole.

He remembered Sadie. She was like a human animal. But what else? What had Sadie done? Why did he know her? How did he know her?

Then his memory was made up of a long period of nothing. Sadie, Gus, then nothing. After this nothing was the compound. A room. A blank room. He met a woman. Doctor Emma Saul.

Then he was leaving. Sadie was dragging him out of a room, taking him to find Gus. He was putting his arm around Gus, helping him hobble out, and the infected were parting, moving out the way for him.

Why did they do that?

Oh, wait.

He knew the answer to that.

Then they emerged. He followed Gus. Did as he was told. Did it as competently as he could. Because that was the plan.

What plan?

The plan.

Oh yes.

"You all right?"

A familiar voice to his side.

Gus. He'd hung back, let everyone else go ahead, to talk to Donny.

Donny didn't know what to say to him. He didn't know what to say to anyone. Still, his mind remained an untouched canvas. An impenetrable fort. No cannon could break down his stone walls, and no knife was sharp enough to penetrate what was underneath.

"Donny, man, I'm talking to you," Gus said.

Donny knew he had to say something.

"Yes?" he tried.

"I asked you if you were all right."

"Oh. Yeah. I'm fine."

"You know, you're kind of freaking us all out at the moment. The way you are. It's strange."

Strange.

Donny was strange.

What was strange?

Was strange being a one-legged man with a feral best friend and a quick-tempered disposition?

"Donny," Gus prompted.

"I'm fine," Donny responded. "Fine. Honestly."

"You're not," Gus insisted. "I can see you've changed. I have no idea what they did to you in the compound, but I bet it was tough."

Donny nodded. He didn't remember.

"They did shit to me too, mate. They tortured Sadie. But, by the look of it, they may have got you the worst."

Donny wished he could be left alone.

"So what did they do?" Gus continued. "I know it's tough, but I really want you to talk about it."

"I'm fine."

"You keep saying that, but you ain't. Donny, you are an irritating guy, but not this kind of irritating. I mean, you're full of life, you're joking all the time, it takes loads to get you to shut up. And now it takes loads to drag out a few syllables. I'll give you time if you need time, but, still, you've got to give me something."

Donny had no idea what Gus was talking about.

Nothing happened. He remembered nothing, so nothing

happened. The time he spent in the compound was locked away somewhere in the confines of his memory, and he neither wished nor intended to access it. The information wasn't required. Not for what he was doing. Not for this.

"Okay, fine," Gus resolved, after a long enough silence. "Just know that when you do want to talk, I'm here."

Gus sped up, walking back to the head of the group to talk to Desert.

Lucy Sanders.

Her name was Lucy Sanders, not Desert.

How did he know that?

Whizzo was a kid from the south west town of Tavistock. He grew up with two parents, had a pet cat. He had done his IT GCSE by the age of eleven. He can take apart and reassemble a computer in under a minute. His real name is Harry Segworth.

Prospero's real name is Luke Worth. His codename, Prospero, was derived from a character in Shakespeare's play *The Tempest*, who was betrayed and left to die on an island, then goes on to free the spirit Ariel – very much like the way he met Desert after he'd been betrayed by Hayes, and helped to free her from the shackles of her persona as Lucy Harvey.

Prospero is proficiently trained as a sniper and is sufficient in hand-to-hand combat.

Donny knew all this and more. He knew everything about these people. Everything except for the reason that he knew this.

He just did. Because it was his job to know.

And it was his job to not tell anyone.

The Journal of Doctor Janine Stanton

Day 3

Transcript from webcam journal by Janine Stanton, third entry

I spoke to him.

I actually spoke to him.

Or, rather, he spoke to me.

Just after I gave him today's dose. Just after my more concentrated solution was implanted into his arm:

40% BLOOD OF MUTATION
15% blood of infected
10% blood of subject
15% ketorolac
10% cortisone
10% water

YOU WILL NOTICE THAT I HAVE AMENDED THE FIGURES rather drastically. Well, I never intended to be using such a quantity of mutation, or pumping in so much blood of infected and, I, er... reduced the other substances. The steroids, the water, they just – seemed to be diluting it too much.

I had no choice.

And, just after I put the needle in his arm, pressed down, that's when he said it.

He didn't look at me. He barely moved, in fact. It was a slow, monotonous tone, a few dry words, and he said – he, he went and said:

"Why are you doing this to me?"

(long pause)

I mean, how willing was he to agree to this? Does he even know what he's doing?

The subject, I mean.

How willing was the subject?

I'm not supposed to call him he. He's the subject. But, then again, isn't that the kind of... alienation... the Nazis intended? Isn't that how dictators, propaganda, all of it – isn't that how they got to where they are? With, with this, blind, utterly blind reign of terror, with legions of followers following blindly, just, completely blind.

I knew there would have been some coercing, I get that. No one would give themselves up to do this without a huge death wish or something. But I never thought someone would be forced into doing this.

I mean – would I put it past Eugene Squire?

(long pause)

I don't know. I don't know how to answer that question. Should I be honest? Is anyone going to see this but me? Surely, if Eugene is the kind of man I'm led to think he is, then this log will be checked and scrutinised and taken apart daily. You know my every action, don't you? You're everywhere.

I mean, it's like you're everywhere.

I don't want to do this anymore.

I never wanted to in the first place. It wasn't like I was given a choice. I thought when I created a successful mutation in the blood that would be it, that was my ticket out, I'd had success, I'd done it, great, send me home, just send me...

But no. There's this. Injecting shit into some guy so brain-washed by whatever Doctor Emma bloody Saul did that I don't even think he knows what day of the week it is!

Then again, do I?

I've been working here so long, I've lost track. Does anyone even keep track anymore? Like, what season it is, what time it is – does it matter? If the world out there has gone to – I mean, if the world isn't what it was, if it is this big, infected pit, then why, why would anyone...

I don't know what the end of the sentence was meant to be.

I've a pretty big hunch Eugene isn't completely innocent in this whole infection outbreak thing.

(shakes her head)

But what exactly am I saying? What am I accusing him of?

I just – I don't know. I, I really don't know what to say. What to tell you. Tell... you, in the sense of this webcam, not the you in the sense that I actually have an audience, that would be... I don't know... crazy. Crazy!

But the whole thing is crazy.

What I'm doing here is crazy.

I'm injecting – injecting infected blood, combined with blood of that girl, combined with shit I thought might make it more tolerable, and it's just, it's doing nothing but aggravating him, I mean, he doesn't react, but I can see it, I see it in the little twitches he does with his eye, like he's trained not to react, so trained, so conditioned that he can't, but he does – it hurts him.

Who even is this guy?

This... Donny Jevon.

Sorry.

The

subject.

No. I won't call him that. That makes it seem like he's not a human being; he is, he is a human being.

At least...

At least, he was, I mean, before he became whatever it is I'm making him become.

(long pause)

Is this my fault?

Is all of this my fault?

Like, should I have never volunteered that synthesis? Should I have pretended it didn't work?

Was I thinking selfishly? Naively?

Like it would make a difference to anything. Like any of this...

Shut up, Janine.

What are you on about?

Just rambling for the sake of it now.

Just... delaying. Going back. Checking on the status of the sub – the human being. The person. The – living – man – that sits in that chair. Without moving. All day, all night. Just sits. Blankly stares.

There's something behind those eyes, I know it. It's just, something's been done to him, something so, so – I don't know. Something so... bad. So mentally scarring. Something that you can't recover from.

(sighs)

Oh, Eugene. What am I doing here?

What are you doing here?

What is the subject doing here?

The man. Not the subject.

Donny.

His name is Donny.

What is *Donny* doing here?

What is the point of this? Of doing this to him?

What is he meant to become?

(long pause)

You know what the worst thing is?

I reckon I know the answer to that question, I just can't bring myself to admit it.

26 HOURS TO TRAP

Chapter Thirty-Two

It was like being awarded a new life. Like being given something remade, that works even better than what was before.

Every step Gus took, every soft sponge into the surface, every pace his new prosthetic limb took, every superbly executed placement of his new foot on the ground – it was like magic. It reacted to the pressure he gave and reacted with the exact amount of precision his body needed.

Even if he still had his leg it would probably have been worth exchanging it for this one.

"How's that baby working out for you?" Whizzo asked, catching Gus staring idly downwards.

It took Gus a moment to realise what Whizzo meant by *baby*. The guy was skilled, but his demeanour was so... youthful.

Only seventeen. Jeeze. So young.

Then again, Gus was already serving in the army at his age. Sometimes you have to grow up fast, and the state of the world must be having such an effect on Whizzo.

I mean, 'Whizzo', he considered. *Surely you could think of a better nickname than that... It sounds like someone who always pisses themselves...*

"Yeah, it's good," Gus replied.

"Glad I went ahead and did it for you now?"

Gus grimaced. The cocky bastard.

Still, couldn't be too hostile – look at what the guy had done.

"Yes," Gus reluctantly surmised. "Yes, I'm grateful. Thanks."

"Welcome," Whizzo replied, completely eluding the word *you're* from the beginning of his sentence. You know, because to say a full sentence would waste way too much time.

Kids.

They travelled on for miles. Gus hadn't moved so much in months, but once he was over his initial stitch, his pride and perseverance kept him going.

Sadie didn't show any fatigue whatsoever. She ran ahead, excited, like his daughter used to do when they were going to a toy shop. Gus knew Sadie was far from cultured or a normal human being, but so many of her childish characteristics reminded him of Laney.

Bizarre, really. How Sadie could have such childish, pet-like qualities, seeking approval and enthusiasm over social activity – yet, at the same time, be as ruthless as she was. Gus knew that, should they be threatened by someone who wasn't infected, Sadie would still not hesitate in decapitating them or destroying them with the gusto she would use against the undead.

Donny was not so recognisable. This guy, who had originally been immensely irritating, who couldn't stop talking at him, still had this expressionless silence, a coldness about him.

Gus knew it would take time. He was a veteran, Sadie was... well, whatever she was. Donny entered this whole façade without any idea about what war was like. This was new to him. And, to have to recover from what they probably put him through, would take time.

Gus decided he was just going to have to be patient.

As they made it through the wilderness, paths entwined between trees, some they had to forge themselves, Gus eventually looked up and saw the sun begin to sink in the horizon.

He caught up with Desert.

"It's going to be dark soon. How much further?" he enquired.

"'Bout another day, I'd say," Desert responded.

"In that case, we should find somewhere to rest for the night. It's getting dark soon, and we don't want to be caught out."

"Fair. Right, shall we say, give it another hour or two, see if we find somewhere we can bunk up – if we don't, we create a camp somewhere? Makeshift shelter with logs or something?"

Gus sighed. It wasn't ideal, but it was the same conclusion he'd come to.

"Yeah. Sounds like a plan."

They walked on for a few minutes of comfortable silence. Gus noticed Desert glancing over her shoulder a few times, her face puzzled, as if trying to figure something out.

"What is it?" Gus asked.

"I – I just – I don't know. I don't get it."

"Get what?"

She glanced over her shoulder again.

"How you ended up with those two. You just seem like such a bizarre group. It's kinda strange."

Gus smiled. He couldn't help it.

"Yeah, I guess it is. One could say we are an odd combination." Gus looked to Sadie, chasing a butterfly. "One could say they saved my life."

Desert went to speak.

Sadie stopped walking, prompting everyone else to stop. She was motionless, like a statue, poised, unmovable.

"What is it?" Gus asked.

Sadie's eyes widened. They turned to Gus.

"The infected?" Gus said.

Sadie didn't move, but her face was his confirmation.

"What do you suggest?" Desert said to him, a sense of urgency compelling her voice.

"It was inevitable," Gus said. "I'm surprised we haven't come in contact with them so far. Get your weapons. We carry on, and we fight any that come."

Groans hovered along the air.

The stench of death caused Gus to flinch.

The rot grew closer. The shuffles along the ground grew closer.

He readied a hunter's knife from the back of his belt.

He turned to check on the others. Sadie was ready. Donny was...

Not there.

Donny was not there.

The infected approached.

Chapter Thirty-Three

Rain.

Soft droplets of bullet water. Gently collapsing, bombarding Donny's skin with its harsh elegance.

He looked to the sky.

He'd had to get away. To be on his own. Get a break. It was tough. Not knowing why he felt so detached, not knowing why he no longer felt anything toward his friends.

Were they his friends?

They were miles behind him now.

He shook himself out of it.

Stop it.

He closed his eyes. Tried to silence the ruthless shouts of his mind. Squeezed every word away from his conscious acknowledgement. Pushed every image to the crevasses of his thoughts, quelled every delusion that questioned his sanity.

He just lifted his face to the sky. To the rain. Pounding him delicately. Brushing him with a mother's touch. It was the only thing that made him aware. Aware of where he was, what he was, what he was doing.

Oh, God, he realised what he was doing.

He fell to his knees.

It all came back. Every droplet another recollection. The things they did to him. The things they told him, branded against his skull, forced into his thoughts.

Gus Harvey. The enemy. The murderer. The neglectful, suicidal alcoholic. He deserved it. All of it.

Except, he didn't.

Gus was his friend.

His *friend.*

Gus had sacrificed...

What?

What had Gus sacrificed?

Why was his memory so distant? Like he was running toward the answer, reaching out and brushing his fingertips, all the while out of reach. Obscured from his...

A sudden cramp in his calf prompted him to fall onto his backside. And then–

His calf.

The pain in his calf.

It all came back. Rushing like a flood that had broken down a dam. Like the rain that grew heavier, the thoughts spread through the rivers of his mind, soaking everything until he was illuminated with the conviction of knowledge.

Cannibals. A family of them. Three. A mum, a dad, a daughter. The dad was dead. Donny did that. He thought he did that. He remembered pointing the gun.

But not the girl and the mum. He remembered his arms being restricted. Like he was restrained. So was Gus. Across from him, so was Gus. Helpless. Like Gus had come back, tried to save him, but then...

Gus did something. What did he do?

What did he do?

What. Did. He.

His calf. A bullet. He had a bullet lodged in his calf. He took it out, put it into a gun, and shot them.

That's how he lost his leg.

Saving Donny.

His body fell. His head buried in his arms, in the mud, weeping. Uncontrollable weeping.

What had they done, that had hidden this memory from him? Such a strong memory, such an important memory. Gone. Hidden. Obscured. Gus had sacrificed the ability to walk. To save Donny's life. To save. Donny. And his life.

He thought back to the facility. To being sat in a chair. A woman injected him. He asked her why. He asked her why she was doing this.

But, that wasn't it – it had come before. Some psychologist.

She had told him stuff.

Boris Hayes.

He had been there.

He had told him who the enemy was.

And the enemy was...

A shuffle in the bushes spurred him to life. He stood. Watched as an infected ran by. Ignoring him.

Gus.

More infected came. Then more. Until there was a horde. Too many to count. All running in the same direction.

A scream.

Coming from across the wooded area. From behind the trees, down the path he had walked.

In the direction that the infected were running.

They wouldn't touch Donny. He wasn't sure why. But they wouldn't.

A scream again.

Sadie.

That was Sadie's voice.

But Sadie doesn't get scared. She can handle herself. Of course she can. So why would she scream?

And how could he hear them?

The infected finished running past him. He saw the end.

And he realised his friends were in danger.

He ran as fast as he could.

Chapter Thirty-Four

They were surrounded. There were too many.

The AGA was dead.

They were all dead.

"Form a circle," Gus said, taking charge, coming up with the only tactic he thought doable.

"What?" Desert responded.

"Let's play this zonally. We form a circle. We're all responsible for the ones coming at us."

"It won't work."

Gus lunged his knife hand and sliced through the jaw of an approaching undead, removing the top half of the ill-fated corpse's head.

"Trust me," Gus assured her. "Okay, in formation, do not break!"

They did as he instructed. He put Whizzo between him and Desert, knowing they would have to pick up the slack; the kid was good with his gadgets, but Gus assumed that combat wasn't his forte. Behind him were Prospero and Sadie. He kept Sadie close – strange, really, why he would feel so protective, when Sadie would most likely be the one protecting all of them.

And on they came. Disordered, chaotic, with speed no man could outrun. From behind trees, beyond the bushes, the rumble of thunder accompanying the rumble of the ground.

Their faces appeared desperate. Cuts in cheeks displayed exposed, decaying jaws, open bellies revealed wayward intestines waving in the wind behind them, greeny-pale flesh from their faces to their hands, finished with sharp, dead fingernails. Their jaws chopped, salivating blood. So many dead faces. So many desperate, hungry mouths.

They were everywhere.

Just everywhere.

Gus sliced through another, stuck his knife into the throat of another, then stuck the knife in the gut of one and unseamed it from its belly to its mouth.

A glance over his shoulder told him that the others were doing similar. Desert was picking up a lot of the slack for Whizzo, who stared wide-eyed, clutching his gun in his shaking hands, shooting in the right direction but at nothing in particular.

Just seventeen, Gus had to remind himself. Just seventeen.

Desert was an expert. She had two blades, one in each hand, and she took her enemies apart with precise lunges, ducks, and swipes.

Prospero was like any typical army general, a look of aged defiance in his eyes, snarling as he shot with deadly aim.

The plan was working. Or so he thought. Just as he turned back, following the split-second he took to check on everyone else, he was already overloaded. Another glance told him that so were the others.

Sadie came to his aid. Just as he sliced through another four, finding more on top of him than he could count, she leapt upon them and ripped them to shreds with her bare hands; landing on their necks, pulling their heads off like rubber on the end of a pencil, then diving into another load, that she ripped apart with her hands and teeth.

Desert saw blood dripping from Sadie's jaw, and immediately turned her gun toward her.

"No!" Gus shouted, hitting the gun away.

"She'll be infected, she'll turn."

"No, she won't, she's immune!"

"What?"

"Just – just trust me."

They fought on, but in seconds they were even more overwhelmed. Sadie was having to take on everyone's fight for them, and it was getting too much. She'd remove another dozen, then another twenty would appear in their place.

"What do we do?" Desert shouted at Gus, backing away from another load that Sadie dispatched just in time.

Gus looked around himself.

He couldn't see beyond them.

And, just as Desert held Gus's eye contact, one of the infected opened its jaw and went for her throat.

Then Gus heard a familiar scream. A scream that changed everything.

Chapter Thirty-Five

The infected halted, still like statues. Desert looked over her shoulder and jumped, abruptly plunging her knife into the head of the nearby infected. But she needn't have. Somehow, all of them had stopped moving – milliseconds from her demise.

Gus breathed a sigh of relief.

He looked around.

They had all frozen.

That scream he'd heard. It continued, persisting as the infected were all hacked down. Heads beyond the nearest heads to Gus disappeared as they fell, and a familiar face appear behind them.

The infected dispersed. All of them, parting out of the way, as if some almighty leader had appeared, as if it was the undead messiah himself.

But it wasn't.

It was Donny.

"Let's go," he said, an air of charm about him. His face was still cold, but there was some expression there, some reaction.

He walked further into the woods and they all followed without question. At least, at first.

Gus didn't take his eyes off him.

The stationary infected, standing still like statues, left their surroundings and wandered into a clearing. Donny led the group along an open field until they were out of sight of the horde.

Gus decided he'd had enough.

"Stop!" Gus demanded.

"We can't stop," Donny answered. "We need to put some distance between–"

"I said *fucking stop!*"

Donny stopped.

As did the others. They all turned to Gus. One by one, Gus saw their faces stare at him. He could tell each of them had questions to ask, but astonishment had prevented them voicing any. When it came to their survival, they all gave their trust to the person who freed them; however bizarre the act of liberation had been.

For Gus, his trust was never up for negotiation. This reeked of suspicion. It made no sense.

Donny was the last to turn. Slowly, after everyone else, he rotated to face Gus. His face was empty, yet full at the same time. Something was different. There was more there, more behind his eyes. Donny had returned, but he hadn't returned the same. That cocky humour had left and was replaced with something far more militarised.

"What is going on?" Gus asked.

"We're escaping."

"That's not what I'm talking about."

"Then what are you talking about?"

"You know goddamn well what I'm talking about."

Desert, Sadie, Whizzo, Prospero. They remained still, tense observers, waiting. None of them objected to the interruption, but none of them dared speak. This was between two old friends.

And they all wanted the answers.

"This," Gus continued. "This... whatever it is. This act of yours. It's getting under my skin."

"There is no act."

"Then where is Donny?"

"I'm right here, Gus."

"Really? 'Cause I don't see him. I just see some scared little prick I picked up from the compound. I don't see Donny. I don't know what you are."

Donny sighed, hesitated, turned his face away.

"Can we do this another time?"

"No, damn it! We do this now!" Gus took a few steps forward. "For starters, where the hell did you get the ability to take those infected down? Last time I saw you, you could barely lift a gun, never mind rip them apart with your bare hands."

"I didn't rip them apart."

"Okay then. What about the way they looked at you?" Gus stepped forward again. "The way they stop moving when you're around. They did it in the compound, and they did it just now."

"Aren't you grateful?"

"Grateful?"

"Yeah! What just happened saved our lives."

"Saved *our* lives?"

"What are you getting at?"

"Answer the question, Donny." Gus had now stepped so far forward he was almost within Donny's personal space. "What happened to you?"

"What do you mean, what happened?"

"Why do the infected stop when you're around?"

"They don't stop–"

"Why, Donny?"

Donny looked around himself uncomfortably. "Look–"

"Why!"

"Gus, man, quit it, I can't–"

"Answer the bloody question!"

"*I don't know!*"

Silence.

Uncomfortable, prolonged, tense, silence.

"What do you mean, you don't know?" Gus persevered.

"I mean, I don't know."

"Just tell us why they do it, Donny."

"I can't."

"Can't or won't?"

"Can't, because I don't know."

"Or won't because you're up to something?"

"Can't because I–"

Donny covered his face. Gus pulled his hands away. Donny was crying.

"What happened to you in that compound?"

Donny covered his face again, shaking his head. Gus pulled his hands away once more. Still crying.

"Quit it, Donny, and tell me – what happened in the compound?"

Donny turned his body away. Gus pulled Donny back, forcing Donny to look at him.

"Please," Donny begged.

"Tell me what happened in that compound."

"Gus, I – I don't know."

Donny fell to his knees. Covered his face. Wept. His body convulsing. He tried wiping his tears away and stopping, but he couldn't stop. He wanted to, but he couldn't.

Gus looked over his shoulder, back at the others. They were all looking at him like they didn't know what to do. All answers eluded them. None of it made any sense.

Gus knelt down, taking Donny's hands away – but this time, slowly. With care. He placed his hand on the back of Donny's head with an affectionate touch.

"Donny," Gus said. "You're my friend."

"You're *my* friend," Donny insisted.

"Then tell me what happened."

"I would if I could, Gus. I really would. I just – I don't know. I don't know. I just know, they were awful things. Really, really, awful things."

Gus nodded.

Donny was telling the truth.

They stayed at the same level for a few minutes, letting the conversation settle, the tension escape, the tears end.

Eventually, Desert tapped Gus on the shoulder and indicated with a nod of the head that he should look at the sky.

It was getting dark.

"There's a farmhouse in the distance, Whizzo saw it through his binoculars. Maybe a mile. We should get moving, before it's so dark we can't see anything."

Gus reluctantly nodded.

He helped Donny to his feet and they kept moving.

The Journal of Doctor Janine Stanton

Day 4

Transcript from webcam journal by Janine Stanton, fourth entry

I...

Jeeze.

(sighs)

I, er...

How do I start?

Honestly, how do I – after that – how do I – how do I even...

(long pause)

I did something stupid today.

Well, stupid's a point of view.

Stupid is as stupid does, my grandma used to say. Then she went senile and tried to eat her own hand. I don't think she's...

(chuckles)

(cries)

I tried to sabotage it. Tried to... to... mess... it all up. To end it. To save this subject – to save *Donny* – from the fate I no doubt believe they have in store for him.

I really don't think he did this willingly.

I think the best thing for him would be to just...

(briefly closes eyes)

So here were the quantities in my latest dose:

. . .

50% BLOOD OF MUTATION

20% blood of infected

5% blood of subject

15% ketorolac

10% cortisone

0% water

I TOOK AWAY THE WATER. INCREASED THE INFECTION. I'LL BE honest, I hoped it would kill him. I'm no murderer, but there's only one way out for this guy, just one way, and that's – and that's–

(closes eyes)

(drops head)

(long pause)

(lifts head)

(wipes eyes)

He didn't turn. But his body – his body changed, somehow. Like it was reacting. Not reacting as in fighting it but reacting as in – changing. Mutating. Moulding the, whatever it is, into something else.

I think I know what I'm doing here.

I think I know what they intend for me to create.

And I think – I think I know what they did to him in the other room. Before. With Doctor Emma Saul.

I read her thesis.

She is an expert in conditioning perceptions. In twisting the way one takes in the world. Making you hate someone you love. Making you decide against your way of life.

She did it with war prisoners. Her PhD, she was turning war prisoners against the opposition and sending them back. Conditioning someone completely against the way of life, their way of life, what they knew, everything they'd become, turning someone against everything they know and everything they–

(pause)

I heard rumours.

There's this place, or group, or something, called the AGA.

I don't know what it stands for, but apparently, they are planning some kind of uprising. Or, at least, they were. They were planning something.

But where are they, then? We've been here for months. Where are they? What's taking them so long?

But, what if the sub– Donny – has something to do with this?

Could he be from the AGA? Could he know of them, could he, I don't know, have something to do with them?

In which case, what are we doing to him? Why are we doing this? And what the hell is it we're doing?

Are we turning him against them? Then sending him back, dosed up on this... stuff... I'm putting into him?

I really think I should have thought this through.

I chose this because I was taking the cowardly way out. I was thinking, do whatever keeps me alive, whatever means they may release me, let me get back to my family, see if they are alive, still there, because I haven't heard from them, and – and – it turned out, I think they probably have no intention of letting me go. I was doing this all under false pretences.

No, I don't think that.

Not any longer.

I *know* it.

I *know* I am never getting out of here.

I should have chosen death.

Yeah, someone else may have taken my place, but I could have taken my research with me. Burnt the room, me in it, my papers, my synthesis, taken all of it down with me. Maybe all the samples they got me from the girl – yeah, they could get more, but it would at least delay them, and then – and then I'd hope that the next person to discover the synthesis I discovered would destroy it too. Would destroy everything. Stop this madness.

It wouldn't last forever. But it would at least last until these AGA people got here. Keep delaying until they arrived, saved me, saved us, saved Donny, done everything they could to kill Eugene Squire.

(shakes head)

Eugene Squire.

Am I too trusting?

Or am I an idiot?

Because, you know what? I'm happy for him to see this.

Yeah, I'm speaking to you, Eugene.

You pompous, psychopathic arsehole.

I'm happy for you to see this.

I'm happy for you to use it as reason to take me off this case, lock me up, kill me, whatever – there is nothing you can do to me anymore. Nothing that will void the shit you've made me do. Look at the person I've become. Questioning myself, questioning everything. I should have questioned it at the start.

I should have...

(bows head)

Why didn't I question it?

(sobs)

Why didn't I...

(inhales)

The subject will wake up soon. I don't want him to be alone.

I best go.

I hate you, Eugene.

I hate you.

10 HOURS TO TRAP

Chapter Thirty-Seven

Gus enjoyed the setting of the sun in the distant horizon for the first time in a while. Strange how it was nature's defects that created the world they now lived in, yet it was nature's beauty that gave them their release.

Everyone was sprinting toward the farmhouse Whizzo had seen, eager to find out whether it would be a hospitable resting place for the night. Gus had noticed, however, that Whizzo had fallen behind, fiddling with something in his bag. Gus went over to see what was delaying him.

"Hey, kid," Gus said. "You don't want to be left behind and get eaten, do you? What's the matter?"

"I'm not a kid," Whizzo replied, still rummaging through his bag.

"Okay, I'll stop calling you kid. I guess you've earnt the right. But you shouldn't stay out here alone."

"I know," the kid replied. "I wanted to show you something. Something cool I've been working on."

Gus looked down at his new leg. Whizzo was undeniably creative, he'd give him that.

"Okay," Gus replied, "hit me with it. What've you got?"

Whizzo opened the bag and pulled out a shotgun – except, it was no longer a conventional shotgun. The muzzle had been widened. The barrel had been tampered with in an obscure way; its shape had been moulded. Attached to the magazine was no space for ammunition, but instead, numerous boxes of lighter fluid held in place. Attached behind that was a box – no, more of a minitank – like a petrol cannister, but smaller.

The thing looked bizarre.

"What the hell have you done to that gun?" Gus asked, bemused.

"This isn't no ordinary gun anymore," Whizzo replied, his face full of pride. "Just you wait until you see."

Whizzo lifted the gun, placed it sturdily on his shoulder, then pointed it at the nearest tree.

"You may want to stand back," he urged Gus.

Gus took a few paces backwards.

Whizzo, grinning wildly, giddy with excitement, took aim and pulled the trigger.

A click sounded, followed by nothing.

"What the..."

He pulled the trigger again.

A click, then a choking. A gurgle from the tank. A splutter of liquid from the muzzle, spewing a few drops that landed in a pool the multicolour rainbow of petrol.

Whizzo dumped the weapon, withdrew a screwdriver, and started taking apart the numerous lighter fluid boxes fixed to the gun's base.

"I take it that wasn't it?" Gus said.

"No!" Whizzo snapped. "No, it wasn't. Dammit!"

He continued to tamper.

"What was it meant to do?" Gus asked.

"It's meant to be a flamethrower."

"A flame thrower? You know, they have already been invented."

As soon as Gus said it, he knew he was being a dick, and urged himself to stop.

"Yes, but this is better. This was going to be a smaller, compact flamethrower, one that we can actually legit carry – yeah, it's got all the stuff attached, but it ain't as big as a flamethrower – but even so, it's meant to be more powerful. Like, have longer bursts of fire, have better aim and a wider landing. It could take out a whole row of the infected, and then fit back in your bag."

Gus couldn't help but admire the ambition. What a weapon that would be – it could take out masses of the infected, assuming that being set on fire was enough to kill them. It would do what would take a far longer period of time to do with a knife or regular gun.

But, let's be honest – this was farfetched. An ambitious project, even for the most resourceful and able minds.

Gus wasn't surprised it hadn't worked.

"Look," he said, trying to be helpful. "It was a nice idea, but maybe you're just being a little, I don't know – too ambitious."

"What?" Whizzo scolded.

"The leg you made me was fantastic, and don't get me wrong, I am so appreciative. But you need both the mind and the resources to do something like that – something many people haven't been able to create. I know my weapons, and I don't know if you would even be able to convert something the size of a shotgun into–"

"Right, okay!" Whizzo snapped. "I get it. You don't think I'm good enough."

"That's not what it is."

"Good. 'Cause you're wrong. I'll make it work. I'll show you."

Gus sighed. Decided not to say any more. It was best just to get them both to safety.

"Okay," Gus said. "You can sort it out later. Let's just get to the farmhouse. We need a good night's sleep."

Whizzo followed Gus, sulking like a stroppy teenager. He had the gun in his hand, tampering with it the whole way.

Then he noticed what it was.

The barrel had been squeezed too tight. That was easy to fix. He could do it, he was sure of it.

But this time, he would wait to demonstrate what he'd created. They all thought he was so useless in a fight, but when he pulled something like this out, he'd show them. All of them.

He'd show them exactly what he was capable of.

Chapter Thirty-Eight

Gus traced the outline of the stars, waving his hand over space, effortlessly touching them with the small pressure of his fingertips.

The farmhouse they'd found was more of a small cottage, one that looked like it had been deserted for a while. It was behind numerous fields Gus assumed were once filled with cattle. The cottage itself was dark and dank, with many corners with many cobwebs and many walls covered with many layers of damp. Moisture hung on the air, and Gus could feel it on his tongue and the dryness of his throat. Its stench combined with the odour of excess mould and dried urine, but he'd had far worse; besides, it was a roof over their head, and it was temporary. As soon as light came, Gus would be waking everyone, and they would be gone. As such, he knew he should get some sleep himself, but his mind was not as weary as his body. Whilst his arms cramped and his leg ached – proving once again that his actual leg was inferior to his new one – his mind was perplexed with thoughts. There were a hundred issues with a hundred possible consequences and no definite answers; barely even any feasible solutions.

"Can't sleep?" came Desert's voice. She placed a reassuring hand on Gus's back, and he returned it with a forced smile. She leant against the windowsill, and Gus continued to stare at the stars.

"I don't sleep much."

"What's on your mind?" Desert asked. A woman who was straight to the point. Gus liked that.

Gus shook his head.

"It's nothing," he surmised.

"It's Donny, isn't it?"

Gus could neither confirm nor deny; which was obvious confirmation in itself.

"What's up with him?" Desert asked.

Again, those hundreds of issues and solutions that eluded him fought his mind. They produced nothing of value, and nothing he could articulate.

"I don't know," Gus concluded.

"I take it he wasn't always like this?"

"God, no. He used to be annoying in a different way."

"How so?"

A distant murmur of groans captured the night air, cutting through its silence.

"He would never shut up. He struggled to have the balls to do what he needed to. But... he was loyal. I gave my leg for him."

"Oh, is that how it happened?"

"Long story, but yes."

Gus sighed. Desert studied his face, half cast in shadow, half covered with a vaguely luminescent glow of the moon.

"We were in that compound for months, though it felt like decades. We were all separated. I was tied to a bed and left to go crazy on my own accord. I have no idea what they did to Donny."

"Was it Eugene Squire doing this?"

"He was involved a few times, but mainly it was lemmings acting on his orders."

"What do you think they did to him?"

Gus shook his head and shrugged his shoulders.

"There's no way to tell. But I saw part of what they did to Sadie, right at the beginning – and they had her chained to the wall, torturing her, and they–"

He interrupted himself, closed his eyes, shook his head, shook himself out of it.

"Whatever they did to Sadie," Gus continued, "they could have done to Donny."

"Then why isn't Sadie–"

"Sadie's not like us."

"Yeah, I noticed that. She had blood on her mouth and she didn't turn. What's that about?"

"She's infected, but she's not changed. That's why Eugene was after her. There's something about her immunity that he wanted to use. It wasn't clear what."

A moment of silence fell between them as Gus's words turned into clarity.

"Donny's never been able to do anything like he did today," Gus said. "Jumping in and ripping them apart, then making them all suddenly stop. It's got me worried. Worried that what they did to him is more than just psychological."

"Is he a liability?"

Gus didn't answer.

"Because, if he is, we need to know now. We can't afford to take any chances. This is too important."

Gus folded his arms, sighed, turned around and leant against the windowsill. He considered the question deeply before producing his answer.

"No, he's not a liability."

"Are you sure?"

"Yes, I'm sure. Donny may have been through a lot, but the guy is still good. Not a bad bone in his body."

Gus smiled to himself.

"I would trust him with my life."

Chapter Thirty-Nine

After trying to sleep for a total of thirty minutes, Gus gave up. His mind wouldn't relax, and, even though he hadn't spent long trying, honestly, he didn't want to sleep. All he'd done for months was sleep to pass the time, and his thoughts were fluttering too fervently around his mind.

Being careful not to wake anyone, he made his way down the stairs, treading softly to mute the creaks of the floorboards. He made his way outside and into the night.

He didn't go far. Just down to the clearing at the edge of the forest, where he paused and took in the cool night air. The air was clean, and it felt good brushing down his throat. The air in the compound had always been so stuffy, so full of the sweat and suffering of everyone in it – fresh air had never felt so welcome.

In a strange way, he wished he had a cigarette. Although that would void the freshness of the air, it just felt right at that time. It wasn't something he'd done frequently, but in Iraq, if you didn't smoke, you didn't socialise. Having a cigarette to give someone when they asked led to conversation that led to solid comradery.

Sighing a deep sigh, he turned and looked back at the farmhouse. Everyone asleep in it.

Except the window at the top, to the left. A figure stood in deep silhouette. Gus could make that body outline anywhere; it was Donny. Yet, even Donny's shadow was unlike him. He didn't stand as he once did; his posture was more... solidified. Definite. Uncompromising. It had an unfaltering confidence that Donny had never previously had.

Gus watched the shadow. Neither of them moved. Gus was sure the shadow was also watching him.

But why?

What was Donny thinking?

Once, Donny's mind would be churning to think of something useless to say. Something daft or stupid or comedic. Like he had to fill every silence with idle chatter about random nonsense. For someone else, that would have been lovely, but Gus had always relished his silence, and Donny had always interrupted it, to great irritation.

What Gus wouldn't give to have that irritation back.

His wife had always loved Joni Mitchell, including one song in particular, *Big Yellow Taxi.* Strange how this made him think of that song, but he found the lyrics somewhat pertinent: *Don't it always seem to go that you don't know what you got til it's gone.*

Maybe Gus had never appreciated Donny for being the person he was.

There was a night, when they were journeying to London under false pretences to save Eugene Squire's child, when Gus had laid with his eyes closed. He'd been peacefully snoozing, but for a moment he'd come around, in one of those strange lapses in sleep when you suddenly become alert, before falling straight back to sleep again.

Donny had been sat with Sadie. He'd always been so good with Sadie, far before Gus ever cared enough to help her.

"Where do you come from?" Donny had asked.

Sadie had looked blankly back.

"Do you" – Donny sighed – "do you have a mum? A dad? A sister?"

Sadie looked as if she was trying to understand, as if some of the words were making sense, but she couldn't form them into coherence.

"Mum? You – have a mum? Dad?"

Sadie raised her eyebrows to show she understood, thought, then nodded.

"Where are they now?"

Sadie looked over her shoulder, then down at the ground. Her lack of answer was enough confirmation for Donny.

"Dead, huh?" Donny concluded, no tact whatsoever. "Yeah, there's a lot of that. You see Gus over there?"

Sadie looked at Gus, who kept his eyes closed, pretending to be asleep.

"His family died."

"Family?" Sadie replied.

"Yes. Gus, family. Dead."

"Oh..." Gus felt Sadie's eyes turn sympathetically to him.

"But he's brave, you see," Donny continued. "Gus. Brave. Because he carried on. Strong."

Gus held his eyes, and a moment of bonding occurred that went deeper than either of them acknowledged.

"Like you," Donny said. "Strong. Like you. To keep going."

Donny looked down.

"I couldn't keep going."

Sadie put an arm on his shoulder, a gesture of comfort, a reassurance he undoubtedly needed. He took her hand and held it, reluctantly smiling.

Gus, despite hating everything and everyone at the time, had let those words sink in.

He was brave. Donny thought he was brave.

That was the last thought he'd had before he sank back into a dreamless slumber.

He hadn't remembered the exchange until a few days later.

Gus looked to Donny now, standing in the window, a silent mystery.

Gus knew Donny was the same person. Whatever happened to him, it had its effect; but trauma does that. Gus only had to look inwardly at himself, at what the death of his wife and daughter had turned him into.

And it took Donny and Sadie to get him out of that.

So it was time he repaid the favour. Letting Donny know who he truly was, so Donny could recover from his experiences.

He'd never thanked Donny, and he never would. Such words didn't come easily to him. But this would be his way of gratitude. This would be the way he solidified that friendship.

He'd remember the Donny that was and hold onto the thought until Donny remembered it too.

Whatever it took.

Chapter Forty

Morning arrived with a rush of sunlight. The heavy rain had parted, if only momentarily, and the spring sun interspersed its light between the shadows, breaking apart the cold of night with the warmth of dawn.

They had already travelled three miles by the time Gus realised how much he was perspiring. It felt oddly refreshing – it was the first time in a while he'd sweated from heat rather than fear. He wiped his forehead with the back of his hand and relished it.

Gus and Desert led the group, eyes alert at all times, ready for anything. Sadie, Donny, and Prospero were behind, and Whizzo took the rear. Whizzo held the radio as tight as he could. He had been trying it continually since they had left the farmhouse. He'd fiddled with the tuning in a way he'd explained but Gus had not understood; Gus's basic understand was that Whizzo was scanning multiple radio frequencies at once, all frequencies to which the rest of the AGA could be listening.

Gus grew slightly perturbed by the lack of contact Whizzo was receiving, especially considering they were supposedly approaching the location. Their imminent arrival left Gus on edge, and although his gun and knife remained in his belt, he kept a hand on each, ready for whatever may come.

"What is it we're looking for?" Gus asked.

"It's an old school," Desert replied. "Like, one that was meant for the worst kids. A pupil referral unit, I think they used to be called. My cousin ended up in one."

"You know, I'm surprised you were once an office worker. The way you fought, the way you hold yourself. You look like you've been fighting this fight forever."

She gave a sneaky smile. "Feels like it."

"I've got something!" Whizzo announced, his voice palpable. "I've got something!"

They all turned toward him, waiting intently to hear the voice through the radio themselves.

"Whizzo, transmission confirmed, over," announced a voice on the radio.

They all cheered, leapt into the air, jumped for elation. Gus and Desert exchanged a triumphant smile.

"Boy, are we glad to hear you," Whizzo confirmed. "I'm going to hand you to Desert, over."

"Roger."

Whizzo passed the radio to Desert.

"This is Desert, over."

"Desert, we thought you were a goner. It's good to hear your voice, over."

"And it's good to hear yours. We're around a mile out, are you ready to receive us, over?"

"Please confirm other survivors, over."

Desert looked at the others. "We have me, Whizzo, Prospero – then we've picked up a few stragglers. Gus Harvey, Donny Jevon, and a girl called Sadie. They escaped from a compound held by Eugene Squire, I can vouch for them."

"Perfect. That's perfect. We'll have someone waiting. Over and out."

"Thank you so much, over and out."

Desert handed the radio back to Whizzo.

"We've done it!" she yelped. "We've actually done it!"

She hugged Whizzo, Prospero, then turned to Gus. Ah, to heck with it, he decided, and he returned her hug, which she then passed on to Sadie and Donny.

"What do you say," she said to everyone. "Shall we run for it?"

They all grinned.

She turned and ran. Gus followed, running freely on his aching leg and his new nimble leg, again relishing the liberation of a perfectly working limb.

The rest followed, keeping up as best they could. Whizzo wasn't much of a runner and almost choked on his breath, but he kept going nonetheless, too eager, too keen to see everyone, to be back with them, to have to do no more fighting – just creating awesome gadgets to help the AGA to victory.

Sadie ran faster than any of them, running ahead, then slowing down to keep the rest of them in her vision.

Prospero enjoyed leaping over random twigs and ducking low-hanging branches.

Donny ran with hesitancy.

Why did he have such a bad feeling in the pit of his stomach? What was it about this place that he couldn't remember?

It seemed important somehow. Crucial. Like he should warn them, do something.

But he ignored it. He didn't know why, but he ignored it. Pretended he didn't feel that way. Knew, somehow, that the best thing would be to just go along with it.

Maybe it was just paranoia. Yes, that's what it was. A lot of what he'd been feeling he needed to ignore. He wasn't well. Hopefully these people would be able to help him.

The group emerged from the trees and bushes and grass and green onto a gravel road. They followed it, and within minutes, they came to a large building. An old-fashioned one, with large, blacked-out windows and a classical brick structure.

Desert reached the door and burst it open, Gus following closely behind. Prospero waited and held the door open for the others.

They entered what must once have been an assembly hall. Where the headmaster would talk to his students. Pass his messages on, and all that.

But there was no headmaster.

There wasn't even any AGA.

Gus stumbled to a stop, as did Desert, as did the rest. Falling. Stumbling. Regaining their footing as their minds struggled to take in the shock.

Gus's entire body stiffened.

How could they be so stupid?

A line of soldiers stood before them, their guns directed forward. Behind them was another line of soldiers doing the same, with another line behind, and another line behind them.

From behind this line, General Boris Hayes emerged, his cocky strut announcing his unmistakeable presence. A grin on his face glowered gloriously.

And, from behind Hayes, came another person.

Someone they all recognised.

Someone with a socially awkward stance that held more authority than it should. Someone with a suit more expensive than he deserved. Someone with a smugness no one could deny.

"Well done, Donny," sang a victorious Eugene Squire, with cockiness that incensed his enemies until they shook with rage. "You led them right to us. You are a good boy."

Chapter Forty-One

Donny was the first to act.

The rest of them stood dumbfounded, dumbstruck, dumb-faced. Looking to one another in an attempt to form a plan with the glance of their eyes, to engage each other into some instinctive strategy of attack.

It didn't work.

Gus's hands remained clutching his weapons, but his weapons remained in his belt. He was outnumbered, it was clear to see. He put an arm out to halt Sadie from bursting forward.

Whizzo backed away, behind Prospero and Desert, as the two stood in a stance mirroring Gus, poised between fight and flight.

Eugene's words hung in the air like the potent stench of betrayal.

Donny was their good little boy. Or, so it would seem.

Desperate to prove them wrong, desperate to go against all the thoughts Donny knew would undoubtedly be flooding Gus's mind, flooding all of their minds, he attacked. He did it alone, but he did it.

He drew his blade and charged at the first line of soldiers.

The soldiers looked to Hayes with an expectant look, a look that asked him what they should do.

Hayes didn't say a word.

He just smiled as he watched his pet unleash the skills Doctor Janine Stanton had injected into him.

The sharp sting of Donny's blade took to the face of the soldier immediately to his left, for the blade to be brought back across the throat of that soldier once more. Blood trickling through Donny's fingers, the soldier fell to his knees and began the prolonged suffering that induced death.

With the element of surprise gone, the next few soldiers lifted their guns.

Donny's speed was such that his actions weren't comprehended until it was too late. A few swift swipes of his hands and the nearest three soldiers collapsed in a bloody mess. Their guns fell to the floor with their fingers. One of them slipped on his own entrails, another grasped at the sprays of blood flying from his gullet, and the other pressed his hands over his eyeballs that boasted a cross in each.

"Donny, stop," said Hayes, raising his hand to halt the rest of the soldiers from further attack.

Donny obeyed with an immediacy that took him by surprise. Aside from his heavy panting, Donny's body didn't falter.

Gus was perplexed. Dismayed and invigorated. Stumped and resolute. Donny was faster than Sadie. Way faster. Sadie was oddly fast, yes, but the way Donny was moving was beyond inhuman. The barbaric swipe of his weapon after the ruthless precision of his speedy attack – it was wrong. It all felt wrong.

"Donny, why are you stopping?" Gus whimpered, loud enough to prompt Donny to turn and look at him.

They maintained eye contact. Donny a sweaty assailant, his

face caught between a snarl and a weep. Gus a confused friend, stuck between shock and horror.

"Donny," Gus said, trying to make his voice louder, only to find himself croak. "How the hell did you do that?"

It was a good question.

How did he do that?

Months ago, Donny could barely survive the easy level on a zombie computer game. Now he could tear three men apart with a single blade in under six seconds.

"I..." Donny tried. "I... don't... know..."

Gus stepped forward, his arm out.

The soldiers gripped their weapons and readied themselves, only to be halted again by Hayes' upraised hand. The smug look on that bastard's face incensed Gus, but Gus was not ready to deal with him yet. He was dealing with his friend.

"Donny," Gus said, "this is... Look at what you've done. I don't even know how..."

Donny was trying not to cry. Gus could see that. A complexity of emotions contorted Donny's features. The realisation of what he'd just done to those soldiers, what he was able to do, and how he understood none of it.

"Impressive," Hayes declared. "Ain't he?"

"Don't you start," Gus retaliated.

Hayes stepped toward Donny, reaching out a hand.

Donny backed away, like an animal threatened by a stranger.

"Now, now, Donny," Hayes said, his arrogance unphased. "Janine wouldn't want you to be uncooperative."

"Janine..."

The name.

The face.

The doctor. The one who was talking to him. Injecting him.

The one who...

He shook his head. He couldn't remember. He didn't know.

"Donny, who's Janine?" Gus asked, but he was ignored.

"And you don't want to let down Doctor Emma Saul, now, do you?" Hayes persisted. "Remember all the things she taught you."

"Who?" Donny innocently replied.

"She taught you about what you had to do. How you had to find the AGA. Bring them here, with your friends. They are here thanks to you."

Desert looked at Gus. "Is this true?" She turned to Donny. "Did you lead us into this trap?"

"No..." Donny whimpered. "It's not true..."

"Oh, but it is," Hayes said. "Only, you don't remember, do you?"

Doctor Emma Saul.

He recalled her face. Her desk. Her title. Expert in psychological conditioning.

Conditioning? What had she conditioned him to do?

"He'd have known nothing about it," Hayes told whoever cared, not taking his eyes off Donny. "But, before it escaped his mind, we planted the thought. We planted everything he needed. The knowledge that he somehow had to ensure you made it here."

"Do you think this infection outbreak was just a mistake?" Eugene interjected with his irritatingly self-important voice. He kept to the side, out of the way of the soldiers. Away from the firing line, where he could remain a coward.

"What?" Gus snorted.

"You think it wasn't engineered? We were trying to create something. Something better."

"What the hell could you create with a bunch of mindless walking corpses?" Gus objected.

"They are the basic level of the infection. The infection has further mutations. Look at your friend Sadie, for example."

They all looked at Sadie. She looked clueless. Unable to understand.

"Her body did what it was supposed to do with the virus," Eugene continued. "When you delivered her to us, she – she was what we needed to know we'd succeeded."

"But you're better, aren't you?" Hayes said to Donny, gradually stepping toward him, his hand still outstretched. "Because we took her blood and we synthesised it and we made it better and we made... you, Donny."

"Don't listen to them, Donny," Gus tried. "Whatever they are saying, you are one of us."

Donny looked to Hayes' outstretched hand.

"You don't belong with them," Hayes continued, ignoring Gus's feeble attempts. "You're better than that."

"Donny, please, come on," Gus urged. "We need you."

"Yes, Donny. They need you. But do you need them?"

Donny reached his hand out and placed it into Hayes's.

"I remember," Donny said. "I remember everything."

"Then you know?" Hayes said. "You know you are ours?"

Donny nodded.

The Journal of Doctor Janine Stanton

Day 5

Transcript from webcam journal by Janine Stanton, fifth entry

Donny spoke to me today. I mean, more than one word. We actually had a conversation.

He asked me what he was doing there.

I told him he was becoming something.

He asked where his friends were.

I told him I didn't know.

He asked if he was going to be important.

I told him...

Nothing. I told him nothing.

I gave the final dose.

80% BLOOD OF MUTATION

20% blood of infected

0% blood of subject

0% ketorolac

0% cortisone

0% water

. . .

SOMETHING HAPPENED. ONCE I DID IT, SOMETHING happened, to him, physically. His body started... throbbing. Like something was crawling underneath his skin. His fists clenched, and he – he changed. He became whatever it was they wanted me to make.

It worked. The damn thing finally worked.

And I created that.

I created that.

And I couldn't believe I did it. So I marched into Doctor Emma Saul's office, I marched in, and I said to her, I said, "What the hell have you done to that boy? What the hell is going on with him?"

She looked back with this smug look like she owned the place and I am not a violent person but I could have gone for her oh I really could have gone for her in that moment I could have – I could have – I could have–

(gathers herself)

She told me to take a seat.

I didn't want to. But I did.

And she explained what she'd been brought in to do.

All of his friends were now his enemies. They had conditioned this into him – through *torture*. Through months of abuse, through pain deterrents, repetition, psychological pushing, whatever barbaric technique there is to mind-fuck someone and change their entire life perception, they did it to him.

They told him where he was to lead his friends to. They told him what he was to do once he got there. They told him that once he'd fulfilled his duty, and he'd taken Boris Hayes' hand, that's when he could remember – that was hypnosis, that one, that technique.

And then, to finish it all off, then they, they – then they made him forget. It all. He has no idea who he is, beyond Donny Jevon. And he gives none of it away. His mouth stays shut, all the time, his mouth stays shut.

Then I came in.

With these stupid injections I convinced myself into doing because I had no idea it would be this bad. I thought I was surviving. But in truth, I'm creating something. I'm creating a... a...

Monster.

Something that can take the infection and turn it into some kind of super soldier.

How did I not realise!

(distant screams)

I knew it was unethical, I knew it was bizarre, extreme, but I had no idea it would be to this extent. Then again, what did I think it would be?

I guess – I guess I thought this was an experiment. I didn't realise I was creating a weapon.

And Emma Saul told me a few more things. She told me that Eugene got some foreign countries to bomb London as a favour, and made it look like an attack.

(more distant screams)

And now he's going to use this guy to create an army to retaliate. That's what they were planning all along.

I ask Emma why she told me this.

(distant screams grow louder)

She just smiled.

She said there's no harm in me knowing, as there is no way I can contact the outside. There is no way I can influence Donny after what she's done to him. And – this one's the biggie, the one that really bites – there is no chance of me ever getting out of here. Not knowing what I know. Nobody can.

(screams outside of room)

Almost as if in perfect coincidence, that's when I heard it. The rumble. I looked out of the window.

There are so many of them.

So, so many.

And they are all running toward us.

The fence – it – it looks like someone has blown it down.

And they are coming.

All of them. They are coming.

(screams outside of room)

(Janine stands, looks off screen)

(loud bang)

(silence as Janine stares off screen)

Are you... are you her?

(silence)

My name is Doctor Janine Stanton.

(silence)

Listen, I don't want to hurt you.

(person appears close to Janine)

(Janine lifts her hand out and strokes hair out of person's face)

Look, I know who–

(person bites through Janine's arm)

(Janine goes off screen)

(Screams)

0 HOURS TO TRAP

Chapter Forty-Three

Donny went to his knee. Bowed his head before his general. Obedient as a lap dog. Pathetic as a wretch.

Gus watched with no conceivable understanding of what just happened. His perception, that Donny was against them, could not be right. This could not be right. None of this could be right.

Yet, as he despaired, watched with distraught eyes, he saw what everyone else saw.

"Good boy, Donny," Hayes said, patronising, cocky, conceited. "You can stand."

Donny stood. His head bowed in a contortion of compliance and reluctance. Submission owned him.

"But, Donny..." Gus tried.

Donny turned away. Kept his face concealed.

"Donny, what the hell are you doing?"

Hayes laughed. "You can try all you want, he's not going to respond to you."

"Donny, whatever they've done to you, you remember who you are, you remember you're a friend, you remember–"

"*Enough!*" Donny's head lifted in a definite twist. His face had changed, showing a look of wrath he had never worn before.

Whoever this was, it wasn't the man Gus knew.

Desert drew her weapon. Prospero already had his out. Whizzo backed further away.

Sadie looked to Gus.

She didn't understand a lot of things, but she understood enough. There was a time to kill the infected, and a time to kill the attacker. The situation was blindingly clear for any onlooker or participant to understand.

"I'm not going to kill him," Gus told Hayes.

"That's fine," Hayes answered. As if to say, *then he'll just be able to kill you.*

Gus drew his blade.

Donny stepped forward, putting himself in front of Hayes.

Out of the corner of his eye, Gus saw Eugene back away. Taking the coward's way. Feeling the fight was imminent, so peeling off to find a good vantage point to watch. Maybe he'll get some popcorn too. Watch the highlights afterwards.

Arsehole.

But Eugene was not Gus's immediate concern.

"Donny, listen, you just–"

"Enough of this," Prospero decided and, before anyone could object or act, leapt toward Donny with his knife showing.

Donny simply sidestepped Prospero's advance and took the man's wrist in his hand. Using strength the muscular former-sergeant couldn't fight, Donny twisted Prospero's knife hand toward Prospero, pressed it forward, and slid the knife's edge neatly into Prospero's gut.

Their eyes met as he did it. Prospero, a face of perplexity, of betrayal, of final thoughts – Donny, a scrunched-up mess of all kinds of anger. His nose curled into a painful grimace, his eyes so full of rage they almost burst from his face.

In a swift motion, Donny withdrew the knife from the gut,

stuck it into Prospero's throat, then kicked the gagging body to the ground as Prospero choked the final few chokes of his life.

"No!" Desert screamed, charging forward. Gus intercepted, placing a hand across her, using all his strength to hold her back.

"Let go of me!"

"You've got to leave emotions out of this. You've got to. Can you do that?"

"Can you?" she asked.

Hayes laughed and clapped his hands.

"Go to hell!" Gus screamed, wrenching his face toward the maniacal sycophant hellbent on wrecking Gus's life.

Hayes just laughed more.

"Why?" Gus demanded. "Just – why?"

Hayes shrugged. "A test that it had worked. Now we can manufacture more of him. An army of them."

"Then what?"

Hayes lifted his arms. "Then... the world."

Donny lifted his blade. Looked into Gus's eyes.

"I won't fight you," Gus told Donny. "I won't. And I won't kill you either."

Donny was not deterred.

Donny marched forward. Gus backed away. Kept his weapons at his side, readily dormant. Donny's strides got him closer to Gus than Gus had precedented, but he just kept backing up, kept getting out of reach.

Gus ran. Ran to a door that led to the old school's corridors.

He looked at Donny, standing there, glaring at him.

If hate had a stench, Donny would reek of it.

Donny looked to Hayes, like a pet to its master, awaiting further instructions.

"Kill him," Hayes instructed.

Gus looked to Sadie, wide-eyed, and pointed at Desert and

Whizzo. "Help them," he told her. "They are friends. Just – help them."

Gus turned. Burst out of the hall, through the corridor, sprinting with as much gusto as his new leg would give him.

He didn't need to turn his head to know that he was being followed.

The heavy footsteps, stomping closer, getting louder, they took over Gus's mind, penetrated it with a strafe of sound.

Gus turned a corner.

The sound of barging against the wall and further running continued behind him.

He turned into a room. An old classroom. What looked like it was a science room; the stools, abandoned Bunsen burners, gas taps all around the room.

Only, this room was it. It was a poor move. There was nowhere else to go.

He shut the door. Backed up against it, pushing it closed with all his might. But, just as the skin of his palm traced the door's wood, the door burst off its hinges, forcing Gus to the floor.

Donny's silhouette filled the door frame.

Gus held tightly onto his blade. Looked like he was going to need it.

Chapter Forty-Four

"Help them. They are friends. Help them."

Sadie fell to her knees. Reached out for him.

His final words before he left. Before they both left. Sadie's two friends. All she had in the world, gone to fight.

"Gus..."

She couldn't understand why. There was no logic to their fighting, no reason she could understand, but they were gone, to hurt each other.

"Gus..."

His final words were not to follow. To help their new friends.

Desert and Whizzo. Their new friends.

Friends.

"Gus..." she sobbed for the last time.

Over her shoulder, Desert backed away.

Whizzo was in the corner. He was rummaging through his bag. Like he was trying to find something.

Before them, rows of soldiers. An army, ready to take them down. Overkill in its most blatant form.

Sadie took to her feet.

She reached her hand out to Desert.

Desert looked back.

"Friend..." Sadie said.

Desert nodded.

"Friend," Desert confirmed.

Sadie turned. Game face on. If she could kill this many of the undead, she could kill this many of the alive.

She knew she wasn't normally supposed to kill people. Gus had said. But this was different.

Gus had said to help them.

And they were in danger.

She scowled.

Hayes laughed. "Look at her, she's like a rat! Or a fucking cat or something. It's pathetic."

Sadie growled.

Desert backed away.

"Right, enough of this. Kill 'em."

The army raised their guns.

Sadie lifted her arms out and screamed. She ran toward the gathering troops. The first spray of bullets hit the ground behind her, unable to trace her speed as she flounced to the left, to the right, and up, jumping over them.

She landed on one of their shoulders. Tried to rip their head off.

But...

Their heads were tougher. They weren't like the infected. They wouldn't rip off so easily. How was she supposed to do this?

She looked to Desert.

Desert was backing away, finding cover behind a large pile of wood, entrails of the school following a likely ransacking for supplies in the initial stages of the infection.

But, just before she found cover, she threw her knife into

the air, at perfect height for Sadie to catch and use to slide into the soldier's throat.

That was better. That went through the soldier much easier.

Desert and Whizzo stayed hidden behind the small barricade. Sadie could see them. More of the soldiers were edging toward them, firing, destroying their shelter, taking away any hope of refuge.

Sadie was not having it.

In a speedy attack, she leapt to the group of soldiers closest to Desert and Whizzo's barrier, taking them to the ground. Their falling caused a few more stumbles of other soldiers, and Sadie used the shelter of the pit of stumbling bodies and momentary lapses in focus to kill a quick sequence of them. Before any other living creature could conceive of the movements, Sadie had swiped her knife through three chests, a leg, two necks, the underside of a chin, and an eyeball; which stuck to the knife, causing her to have to wipe it off on her trousers.

Icky.

She ran toward the next load of oncoming assailants, diving into them, moving her knife hand quicker than they could react.

So quick, she didn't even hear the gun fire before it got to her.

Her shoulder. Immense pain. Then a sudden feeling like she was drowning.

She fell onto her back.

She heard someone scream her name, probably Desert, possibly not.

She howled. It was agony.

The soldiers parted. Allowed the shooter to walk through.

General Boris Hayes, his jacket off, his gun out. Doing what he did best. Striding like Moses, arrogantly marching through the parted sea of soldiers.

Sadie dragged herself back to her feet, went for him, but

stumbled, her balance gone, the pain taking over any movement she attempted.

Hayes aimed the gun at her face.

She swiped for it, but missed, falling, collapsing in an earthquake upon solid tiles.

That was when Whizzo stood and withdrew something from his bag.

Chapter Forty-Five

Gus crawled backwards along the floor, staying beneath the concealment of tables. He knew it wouldn't protect him for long, but every action was an immediate thought; once he'd been afforded the next few seconds of protection, he'd produce the next.

Donny threw the tables out of the way like they were nothing. Sent them surging into smashed windows to his right, faded displays to his left.

He kicked the chairs, sending them spinning across the room, punching the far walls with a heavy dent.

"Donny..." Gus began, then decided to stop.

He hadn't been able to rationalise with Donny so far.

Could his friend be so far gone?

Gus knew he had to find some way to stop Donny without killing him.

Or, failing that, he wouldn't have a choice. He would have to...

No. He couldn't kill Donny.

Only, Donny's blood had what Eugene Squire needed. It had the blood of what they were trying to create.

For the greater good, there was no way Gus could let Donny go.

For his own breaking heart, there was no way Gus could let Donny die.

Gus ran out from beneath the final table. He fumbled to his feet, using a nearby sink to steady himself. His head was smacked into that sink before he had any idea it was about to happen.

He ignored the delirium and pushed himself hazily back up, running, just running.

He saw a back door. There was a back door. A means of escape. A means of not dying.

But it was so far away. Metres, yes, but in terms of–

His lamentation was cut short. Donny gripped Gus around the throat with his firm hand and lifted him into the air. Gus grabbed Donny's wrist, squeezing, pulling, trying to tear it away, but Donny was not interested. He even tried kicking Donny. Fighting back seemed like the only way – for now. But his kicks may as well have been done by a toddler, such were their effect.

He choked. His breath. Escaping.

Gus lifted his hands into the air and brought them down on Donny's elbow with all the weight he had. Donny's arm capsized long enough for Gus to free himself and run.

Gus's respite didn't last long as Donny leapt to a table, perched on it, then launched himself toward Gus, taking him to the floor.

Gus made it back to his feet, only for his face to meet the strike of Donny's fist.

Another strike came, and Gus blocked it. Before he could relish his success at blocking the punch, he felt the surge of anguish tremor up and down his arm, reacting to the force of the punch.

He blocked another with his other arm, then another with the original arm.

They ached. Ached like hell.

Upon the next block, Donny opened his fist and grabbed the arm that Gus attempted to block with. With the temporary setback delaying Gus's thought process, Donny swung his other arm into Gus's face. The impact sent Gus off his feet and into the chalkboard behind him, thousands of particles of dust spraying into the air.

Gus made it to his feet and used both hands to block another punch. He took Donny's striking wrist in and tried twisting it. As he did, his face grew closer to Donny's.

"What are you doing, man?" Gus asked. "Just stop and listen to me."

Donny's face was not his own. It belonged to fury.

Donny simply over-muscled the hold Gus had, firing his fist through Gus's stomach.

Gus coughed, winded, but did not make the mistake of being still. Avoiding this complacency allowed him to run to the backdoor.

Rain thudded the window of the backdoor, but it did not make Gus hesitate; if anything, the rain would help to complicate things for the opponent. And, although Gus knew that the speed at which Donny seemed able to fight and process his next move would not be faltered by the pounding bullet-drops of weather, Gus had to take whatever delusional optimism he had and hold onto it.

Otherwise, the fight was completely lost.

Gus reached the backdoor, stretched his hand out for the handle. He didn't make it. The heavy impact of Donny's foot sent him through the glass. Gus had no idea it had happened until he was pushing himself to his knees, registering the sting of multiple shards stuck to his body.

He pushed himself to his feet once more, brushing the particles away, wincing as the tiny pricks left small spots of blood staining his skin.

The rain hit him. Hard.

He fell back to the floor.

Everything on his body hurt.

As he looked up and saw Donny approaching once more, he understood what was going to happen.

He was going to lose.

Hayes was going to win.

And Gus was going to die.

Chapter Forty-Six

It felt heavier than Whizzo. And if it weren't for the fact that it had fit in his bag, from looking, you would presume that it was as big as him, too.

It used to be a regular shotgun. Now it was bigger. Attached to it were various wires leading to various small boxes of lighter fluid, with a larger tank on the reverse of the shotgun.

Gus had been impressed by the ambition, but not so impressed by its progress.

Well, it was unfortunate that Gus was not going to be there to see it in action.

Whizzo just hoped it was going to work this time.

Hayes peered bizarrely at the object Whizzo lifted. He was torn between raising an eyebrow, guffawing, and demanding to know what it was.

But one plus one soon became two, then multiplied into equations of fear.

"The lighters..." Boris muttered. "The tank you attached... is that..."

Whizzo smiled. He didn't need to say what it was. He just needed to pull the trigger.

"Desert, Sadie, duck," Whizzo said, Desert looking just as confused as the opposition. She whipped herself to shelter, grabbing Sadie's arm and taking her with them.

Hayes went to call for his troops to back away, then stopped. If he did that, they would all run for it. If he didn't order them to flee, he could escape first and put all their bodies between him and it.

So that's what he did. Turned and ran, shoving soldiers out the way.

Before any other soldier could object or run or voice any concern, Whizzo unleashed. Pressing firmly on the trigger, which had required far more pressure than the gun would have before, he sprayed and sprayed steady streams of flames.

The soldiers backed up, but for the front line it was too late. Some fell and rolled, unable to batter the fire from their bodies. Some were incinerated immediately and fell in a black, sooty mess. Some even turned and ran, alit, spreading their flames to the other soldiers.

Desert loaded her ammunition and took Whizzo's side, along with Sadie.

"Together," she told them. "Let's move."

Side by side, they walked forward, placing each firm step one after another.

Whizzo would go first, pushing a line of fire amongst the fleeing soldiers. He would take out the nearest bodies, then, as he waited for the rest of the petrol to flow from the tank to the gun, Desert would see to any strays, pointing her gun with pinpoint precision and ploughing the pathetic morsels who still hadn't burnt to a crisp. Following this, Sadie would jump on any that had somehow missed the attacks and end their suffering with more suffering.

"Keep going," Desert urged him.

The soldiers were fleeing out the door. There were few left.

They stepped over bodies as they persisted, continuing forwards.

Desert looked down. At the features on the scorched faces around her feet. The uniforms. Scanning their features. Searching for the face of General Boris Hayes.

"You carry on," Desert urged Whizzo and Sadie, then carried on searching, eager to see if they'd tagged their commander.

Whizzo did as he was advised.

Another elongated spray of fire was all it took to see off the final few attempting to retreat. There were no more stragglers for Sadie to pick off. As the last few bodies fell to the ground, the last few screams sounded from those being twisted to death by heat. He dropped the gun to his side and waited.

He wasn't sure what for.

For them to return, maybe? Cancel their retaliation?

But no. He could hear the mass of footsteps from those few lucky enough to survive, making it out of the building. They grew faint, and Whizzo became fairly certain that they were alone.

He turned to Desert, who was walking up and down the tatty corpses decorating the floor of ash. Her eyes scanned each body, and her face look troubled, as if she wasn't satisfied.

"What is it?" Whizzo asked.

Desert put her hand up, asking him to wait as she continued searching.

Whizzo looked at the empty visage of a nearby body. He did that. He had done that. All of it. Their death was on him.

He threw up. It was uncontrollable; a mouthful of bloody sick lurched to his mouth and landed over the blackened trouser leg of the nearby body.

Desert met his side.

"I know," she said. "It sucks."

"I – I – I..."

She placed a reassuring hand on his shoulder.

"If you hadn't done it, we'd be dead. These were the bad guys."

Sadie put her arms around him. A hug was probably the best that she could offer. He'd take it.

Still, Desert seemed distracted, peering at the various corpses.

"I can't..."

"Can't what?" Whizzo asked.

"Can't see them. Eugene Squire and General Boris Hayes. Their bodies aren't here. They escaped."

Chapter Forty-Seven

Loyalty was nothing. In the clarity that arrives with imminent death, your need for survival grips you with a fever that will not let its sickness go.

That was Hayes's reasoning.

As far as he was concerned, most of this army were dead. They weren't that great, anyway.

He didn't need them anymore.

They weren't anything like the army he was going to be able to produce now.

Donny Jevon, the little miracle. His blood contained the synthesis needed, and they would use it, inject it into tens, hundreds, maybe even thousands. He would create the most remarkable army the world had ever seen, and there would be no army that would be able to outdo them.

Donny had everything. Speed, muscle, awareness, aggression. That Sadie girl was nothing compared to what they'd produced.

He could see it now in the perfect simplicity of his mind's image. All of them marching under his command. Other countries falling by the wayside, dropped into the gutter on their way to greatness. It was beautiful. Glorious. Divine.

"Boris!"

A distant voice. Like one in the back of his head. Silently screaming.

What was it?

"Boris!"

Was he imagining it? It was getting louder.

It was kind of posh.

It was...

"Boris!"

Ah, yes. Of course.

Hayes turned and spotted him straight away. He was the bumbling idiot amongst a horde of charging soldiers. Muscular, kitted-out troops barging forward, then this little dweeb of a man jumping up, getting knocked about, pushing his way through them.

"Boris!" Eugene yelped again.

"Quick!" Hayes demanded.

After being knocked out of the way by a few more soldiers, Eugene eventually reached Hayes' side.

"What do we do?" Eugene asked. The prime minister like a timid child looking for orders.

"Do?" Hayes repeated.

"Yes, what should we do? We've lost!"

Hayes laughed. Stood still, cackling amongst the constant stream of troops.

"We ain't lost, Eugene," Boris cockily insisted. "We are nowhere near lost."

The last of the soldiers left, leaving one remaining vehicle and the pounding rain.

"But – didn't you see?" Eugene continued.

"I saw a guy with a freak invention scare a bunch of pansy soldiers. I didn't see no one win."

"Boris, I – I – I don't quite understand."

Hayes placed a strong hand on Eugene's shoulder, making Eugene flinch from the slight crush of Hayes' grip.

"Eugene, don't you see? Donny Jevon was the thing we were trying to create. Did you see him?"

"Yeah, yeah I did," Eugene responded, cheering up.

"Did you see what he could do?"

"Oh, boy, did I."

"Imagine an army of them. Imagine it. We don't need a bunch of deserters who run at the small sign of trouble – we need an army of *him*. And we'll have it. Now that we've seen what we can make, we'll have it."

Hayes straightened up. Looked to the far window, where a commotion was being created. Smashes and crashes caught the disrupted sky in its extremity, punching through the heavy thunder and ripping wind.

"Well," Eugene said, "shall we go?"

"Not quite yet."

"Why? We have a car!"

"Yes, but, Eugene – we also need the boy's blood."

Hayes withdrew his handgun.

"Are you going back in there?" Eugene asked.

"You can wait in the car. I'll be out with the boy in ten minutes."

His eyes focussed ahead. Vision hellbent on the commotion, he took his definite strides forward, making his way without faltering to where his prize was beating Gus Harvey to death.

Chapter Forty-Eight

Some think that rain is just an element of weather. That rain is simply particles of water created by clouds to disrupt our daily lives.

No. This was what rain was created for.

As Gus backed away, crawling along the soaking surface, leaving the pavement for the soft soil of a flower bed, Donny towering over him, water pelting his face without mercy, Gus wondered if the water thudding against the ground would be the soundtrack to his betrayal.

Rain was made for betrayal. For hate, for anger, for friends lost and never to be found again. It was a scene like this where rain came into its own. Became more than a passing annoyance or gentle tapping against the window; it became a prominent weapon of the sky, a thunderous battering of its harsh sting adding danger to any regular surface.

Donny placed his rough paw around Gus's collar and lifted him into the sky.

Gus retracted his fist and launched it into Donny's face, again, and again, and again.

Donny barely winced.

He threw Gus into the mossy brick wall and, as he landed, Gus was sure he could feel something crack in his lower back.

Donny went for Gus again, but Gus, predicting the move, jumped up and ran, moving further into what was once a playground, and what was now a soggy mess covered with calamity. Drawings on the floor of ladders and games like hopscotch faded into faint chalk outlines, Gus's ankles growing muddy against the splash of puddles.

He sprinted, moving his arms up and down, his thighs doing most of the work, a succession of movement designed to escape.

Then what?

As he ran, the question Gus had neglected formed with unmistakable comprehension.

Was he just going to keep running?

There were only more walls at the end of this playground. Only more classrooms for him to run into. Was he just going to keep running?

No.

He stopped.

He turned.

He faced Donny, who merely marched toward him, the width of his paces carrying him closer with ease.

Gus couldn't fight Donny.

Gus couldn't run from Donny.

Now what?

"Donny!" Gus shouted.

Donny was undeterred.

"Donny, stop!"

Donny's face suffered a brief flicker of perturbance, a frown that showed how little he was bothered.

"Donny, please, man, you got to listen to me," Gus beseeched him.

Gus's whole life, he'd fought. Fought against his teachers, his parents, his enemies, even his friends; the few he'd had, however fleeting those friendships were. He'd fought against the dictatorship of Saddam Hussein, he'd fought against the Taliban, and, more recently, he'd even fought against his own oppressive government.

He'd fought the infected. He'd fought those closest to him. He'd even fought himself.

This was the time that fighting stopped.

This was the one time he would not win with his fists or his blade or his bullets.

So what else was there? What else did he have?

Donny slowed down, approached Gus with a sneaky slant in his smirk, a knowing look; a look that said the power was his and all it would take was one swipe.

"Please, Donny, you're only doing this 'cause of what they done to you. It ain't real. It ain't. You just got to–"

Gus bowed his head. Ran his hands over his face and through his hair.

When he looked up, Donny was holding his arms out mockingly, as if to say he was awaiting this great speech that was going to entice him to stop.

Gus went to speak.

But what could he say that hadn't already been said? Already been thought? Already fallen on ears that would rather not listen?

"What about Sadie?" Gus tried. "What about her?"

Donny sauntered closer, still wearing that infuriating smile.

"Sadie is the one who made me go back for you. When those cannibals had you, I was done, I was going to leave. But she's the one who made me turn back."

Donny withdrew his blade.

"If it weren't for her, they'd have eaten you, and you wouldn't be here right now, doing this to me. There wouldn't be any of this."

Donny punched a nearby classroom window, smashing it into fragments. He peeled away the biggest slab of glass he could find and inspected its sharpness.

He picked up the pace of his walk, holding the lethal point by his side.

"In truth, I'm glad she did," Gus tried. "I am. 'Cause you taught me so much. You taught me about putting up with people who piss me off. How they aren't all that bad." Gus laughed. "Because boy, did you piss me off, especially at first. Probably even more than you're pissing me off now."

Donny's sarcastic grin left, replaced by a face curled with hostility.

"And now you're going to kill me."

Donny charged, holding his weapon in the air, ready to strike.

A FEW MONTHS OR SO AGO

Chapter Forty-Nine

A peaceful half-crescent moon paraded itself proudly in the sky. Its calm serenity fed through Gus. He liked the night, always had. Its dark concealed the shadows, its tranquillity hiding the bustle that was caused by everyone being awake.

"Hey," came Donny's voice behind him, startling him.

Oh, great. Company. Just what Gus didn't want.

This whole expedition to rescue this little girl, going into the pit of the infected that was London, risking his life, that was fine; it was the company he could do without.

Still, Donny had shot a gun for the first time for Gus. He had finally been useful.

Maybe he should cut the kid some slack.

"What's up?" Gus asked.

"Not much. Mind if I join you for ten minutes or so?"

Gus sighed. Did he have a choice?

"Go for it."

Donny walked over and sat down on the grassy verge beside him. Across a few trees and a few bushes, he could see Sadie asleep, her chest rising up, her mind escaping into her unconscious state.

"I'm sorry about earlier," Donny blurted out.

"What you sorry for?"

"Well, me, not shooting the gun – it was dangerous. It put us all in danger. It was... stupid."

Gus shrugged. "First time shooting a gun, not hard."

"Yeah, but at one of the infected. It wasn't even a person, it was one of the friggin' zombies."

Gus snorted. Zombies. Felt crazy to call them that, but that's what he guessed they were.

"It was always so easy on my computer game," Donny stated.

"Oh, yeah, you like computer games?"

"Love 'em."

"What's your favourite?"

"*Quake. Halo*."

"Halo? Ain't that old now?"

Donny shrugged. "I love the retro stuff. Feels nostalgic."

"I used to play that before my kid came along."

Gus bowed his head. Why did he have to mention his daughter? He hoped Donny didn't ask any further questions.

"You must miss them, huh?"

Dammit.

"Yeah."

A moment of lingering silence hung between them.

"I can't sleep. I just keep thinking of how I screwed up. I just – I'm so sorry, Gus."

"Just shut up about it, yeah?"

"But–"

"Just–" Gus raised his hand. Donny fell silent.

They sat in silence. After the silence had been too prolonged, Donny reluctantly went to get up.

"I'm sorry I disturbed you, I–"

"I envy you," Gus interrupted.

Donny didn't move. Turned back.

"You what?"

Gus sighed.

"When I first had to kill one of those things, when I saw it change, when I saw it go to bite someone, I didn't even hesitate. I didn't even cough. I just did it. That's the worst thing."

"Yeah, but you were ruled by instinct," Donny said. "And you had the guts to go with what you thought was right. What you knew was right."

"No, it weren't nothing like that. I just saw them, thought, them or me, and did it. First time in the army I had to kill a man, it kept me awake for a few nights, then the next one, it bugged me for ten minutes, then the next one... Didn't even register. I went back and had my tea and slept soundly."

"But they were the enemy."

"Yeah, it's still a life. And I hate how easy I find it to take one. And I envy how tough it is for you."

Donny's head dropped.

"I respect you for it," Gus said, standing. "I do. I really do. But next time – pull the trigger. Living is worth a few sleepless nights."

Gus went to walk away, then paused, turned back to Donny.

"Hey, kid," Gus said.

"Yeah?"

Gus forced a smile.

"You're all right."

Gus meandered further into the woods on his walkabout, leaving Donny stood there, undecidedly chuffed.

Why he was chuffed, he didn't know.

He hadn't craved Gus' respect. He had wished to have a civil conversation, but he hadn't sat around thinking that Gus and he should be best friends.

But, now that he had the man's respect – he felt like it would be something he would hold onto until the day they died.

THE TRAP

Chapter Fifty

Gus blocked the initial strike from Donny's hand that held the sharp, broken shard of glass. Gus knocked it into a nearby puddle.

It didn't deter Donny. He didn't need it. Gus failed to block Donny's fist as it launched forward and planted itself through Gus's face.

Immediately, Gus felt his nose crack. He fell to the floor faster than he was able to comprehend. He closed his eyes, shutting out the pain.

Donny lifted Gus by the collar once more and laid his fist right back into that face, sending Gus soaring back to the wet surface.

It went blank for a second, but Gus kept his consciousness. His awareness was going, but that was fine, he could survive without it; it was his consciousness he needed to retain.

Gus didn't bother getting up. He stayed on his back. In the distance, Desert and Whizzo appeared. Whizzo had some big gun.

Gus held his hand up, slightly, just enough for Desert and

Whizzo to notice, but Donny not to register. They halted, and he locked eye contact with them and shook his head.

This was a fight he had to do on his own.

He knew, just as well as they did, that if they entered the fight it would be to kill Donny. Gus knew what Whizzo was holding in his hand, and he knew what it could do.

Whatever happened, Gus would not let one of his few friends in this world die – even if that friend was pummelling him to the final inches of his life.

Donny's fist soared downwards once more, causing Gus's slightly raised head to jar against the cement. Blood mixed from the back of his head, diluted by a puddle.

His eye blinked. He could not longer open it. It had been battered shut. His other eye, he could just about lift his eyelid.

"Donny..." he tried, but it came out in a wheeze, barely audible against the rain's savage bombardment.

Donny lifted his arm back once again.

Gus winced, readying himself for impact. Would this be it? How many punches was it going to take to kill him?

"Donny!" came a voice from across the playground. "Donny, come on!"

Donny's head turned, as did Gus's; though Gus had to turn his head further to direct his one good eye.

General Boris Hayes stood at the far exit, waving Donny onward.

"Finish him off, we need to go!" Hayes shouted.

Great. Just what Gus needed. *Now Hayes is here to watch my best friend murder me.*

Gus had always wondered how he'd go. Honestly, for the longest time he'd been sure it would be suicide. Then, he thought it would be starvation in the compound. Now, here was his answer.

"Let's get on with it, we need to go!" Hayes insisted.

Donny turned back to Gus.

"Please..." Gus begged, forcing the croaks of his voice out.

Another strike, another eye gone.

He could just about open it, but it didn't matter, everything was a vague blur. If the rain didn't obscure his peripheral vision, his hazy mind would.

So he kept his eyes closed. He didn't need them.

"You know what you once said you respected about me," Gus began, shouting so his voice would be audible.

He felt his collar being lifted. He didn't bother wincing. The next strike was coming either way. He just relaxed, flopped his body.

"You once told me that you respected me," Gus said, "because I had the guts to do what I knew was right."

He felt his body dangle under the strength of Donny's grip on his collar.

"Because I knew who to kill and who not to."

He waited.

"And I respected you for finding killing to be so tough..."

He waited some more.

Waited for the impact. The imminent punch.

He waited and waited.

It was not forthcoming.

He was just left in limbo, held by the collar, awaiting his fate.

"You said that..."

He spluttered. Coughed up a bit of blood. Spat it out.

"Living is worth a few sleepless nights."

He heard nothing but the rain. Felt nothing but the rain. Beating his body.

"That killing was tough for you, and that..."

He choked up another bubble of blood.

"That is why I won't hurt you. Because you – *Donny* – are the kind of person I envy."

He sniggered to himself. Tried to open his eyes, but it still hurt too much.

"You're the person I wish I was."

He stopped talking. Rested his voice.

Waited for the final strike.

The final curtain.

The final full stop.

But it never came. That curtain stayed open, the sentence left incomplete.

The grip on his collar loosened and he fell. Hammered back down to earth.

His clothes were drenched, but he hadn't noticed it until now. His whole body was soaked through. A cold breeze flew in and made him shiver.

But there was nothing else.

He listened.

Nothing.

"Donny?" he asked.

The patters of nearby feet arrived at his side.

He tried to open his eyes, but it was too painful. He let them stay shut.

"Donny, is that you?"

"No, Gus," came Desert's voice. "It's us. We're going to help you get out of here."

"Where is Donny?"

A long pause ensued.

"Where is he?"

"He – he left, Gus," Desert answered. "He left with Hayes."

Gus smiled. "Good lad."

"What do you mean, good lad?" Whizzo interjected. "He left with the enemy. He betrayed us, he led us here. How on earth is he a good lad?"

"Because... because he didn't kill me."

He attempted to hoist himself up, and that was when he finally allowed himself to fall unconscious.

TWO WEEKS LATER

Chapter Fifty-One

Once again, Gus woke from a long sleep. Like before, a mixture of physical exertion and taking a harsh beating had forced him into a vaguely comatose state. At least this time he was not restrained to a bed; nor did he have Eugene Squire's smug face standing over him, and no stick-up-his-arse guard waiting outside the door.

Just Desert, sat serenely in the chair next to him.

"Where am I?" he managed, looking around his blank chambers. His eyelids were sore, but he could at least open them.

"A black site."

"A what?"

"It's a safe house for the AGA. We had nowhere else we could go, we had to bring you here, but we can't stay. We don't know what they know, it might not be safe. Please gather yourself. We'll leave as soon as we're able."

Gus leant his body upward, looking around the room. It was like a tin can, some kind of bomb shelter. From the lack of windows, he assumed it was underground.

He sat up, placing a pillow behind his back and leaning against the wall.

"How long have I been out?"

"Weeks. You haven't been entirely gone. You've dipped in and out a few times, but this is the most we've gotten from you since we got you here."

"Aw, man," he muttered, rubbing his forehead. He had a pounding headache.

As he turned and looked at Desert, he saw a look of... annoyance, maybe. Irritation. Despondency mixed with the vacant glare of a grudge.

Come to think of it, her voice had been steadily monotone so far, very matter-of-fact. Something was clearly irking her.

"What's the matter with you?" Gus asked, still readjusting to being awake.

"What do you think is the matter with me?"

"I haven't the foggiest."

"We had him with us the whole time. He travelled from our original hideout, to the main headquarters of the AGA – hell, he probably gave away where we were heading."

Gus shook his head at her. Abhorrently perturbed. How dare she?

"You think this ain't affected me?" Gus retorted.

"Don't start."

"Donny was a friend – besides Sadie, my *only* friend. I'd give anything for him. Then he threw us under the bus and beat me half to death – do you really think I ain't pissed, too?"

"He killed Prospero!"

"And how could I have seen that coming?"

"You brought him to us, we didn't bring him to you."

"That's not–" Gus stopped himself. He was shouting. He lowered his voice. "That's not here or there. You think I could have predicted this?"

"From the way he was acting, if it was so different from the norm – yes."

"For Christ's sake, Desert, we'd just spent three-odd months in a compound being tortured. Hell knows what they might have done to him in there. I thought he was bound to have a reaction, there was no way I could have predicted *that*."

"Well, you should have."

Gus nodded sarcastically, then returned to his headache. He could do with some paracetamol or something – but, in the apocalypse, such frivolities were rarely forthcoming.

"So, what now?" Gus asked. "You done with us? We go our separate ways, that what it is?"

Desert shrugged. "You're the closest thing we have to allies now. As pissed as I am, I don't know if I want to abandon that."

"Well I ain't really much up to being no one's last resort."

"It isn't a last resort. It's an only resort. And we're yours."

Gus raised his eyebrows at her, an action of hopelessness mixed with a lack of ideas.

"We only stand a chance of overthrowing the government if we are together," Desert persisted.

Gus scoffed. "We don't stand a chance, Desert."

"We–"

"Did you see Donny? See what he could do? They are building a whole army of him. What are we supposed to do about that?"

"Then we need to stop them before they make that army."

"Do you think I'm not pissed? There was stuff you didn't tell me. Like this whole super-soldier creation, this whole background to the whole outbreak – ring a bell?"

Desert shrugged. "I guess we both have our faults."

"Ain't that the truth."

Desert sighed. Leant forward. Placed her elbows on her knees and her chin in her hands.

"So you going to help us or what?" she asked.

"Let's make one thing clear. I only care about Donny. I'll help you get in, get at Eugene and Hayes and all that, but once we're there, I'm rescuing Donny. That's it."

"It doesn't look like Donny wants to be saved."

"He ain't himself, all right? He will be saved. And I'll be the one to do it. And that's how we'll help each other."

Desert took a moment to contemplate this.

"Deal."

"Great."

Desert felt for his leg. He'd forgotten he only had one. The prosthetic still held in place, a sturdy creation.

"So," Desert asked, her voice with a renewed friendliness. "Do you really think we can stop them before they create that army?"

Desert looked at him, waiting, expectant of an answer.

He didn't give her one.

Chapter Fifty-Two

Eugene and Hayes lifted their glasses of Eugene's Remy Martin Louis XIII cognac and toasted their success.

"Bloody marvellous!" Eugene declared, and drank his brandy in one go. "Absolutely bloody marvellous."

"I have to admit," Hayes replied, sipping on his brandy, "I was pleasantly surprised."

"You mean you doubted it?" Eugene said, playfully ironic.

"Oh, never, of course. But I did wonder. About whether we'd done the right thing sending him off and out of our sight. Whether what Doctor Saul did would stick. But it did. Oh boy, it did."

Eugene placed his glass on a drinks mat with the St. Georgie's flag on that sat proudly upon his pristine wooden desk.

"What now?" Eugene asked.

"I'll show you," Hayes replied, a cheerful twinkle glinting in the corner of his eye.

"Oh boy, oh boy, oh boy!" Eugene said, doing all he could to contain his childish excitement.

"Come with me."

Hayes led Eugene out of his office and down the corridor. As they did, they saw Eugene's transmission on the televisions in the passing offices. All televisions had been cut off for over a year, and his smug face was the first transmission to be made after all that time. Magnificent.

"Ooh, one moment," Eugene said, putting his hand out to Hayes. "I want to see this. How do I look?"

"Good evening, United Kingdom," came Eugene's voice on the screen. "As you may be aware, almost five months ago, bombs were dropped on London. There has been a rumour that this was our allies helping us in destroying the quarantined zone where most of the infected live."

Eugene clapped. The best bit was coming up.

"Following the sad state of affairs in our beloved country, it only makes me unhappier to have to give you the bad news that this rumour is unfounded. As far as we are aware, these countries believe that we are responsible for the infection, and this was their retaliation. This ruthless bombing was no more than an act of terror, intended to wound what is an already bleeding Britain. As a nation, we must stand stronger, together. We will react. Our troops are readying themselves as we speak, and our enemies should ready themselves for war."

It was like a new kind of masturbation. Eugene loved it. His face, announcing his glorious lie to the gullible nation. Everything he'd planned was coming to fruition. It hadn't been easy to begin with, but here it was. Forming perfectly.

"What do you think?" Eugene asked.

"I think you need to see that army you're going to retaliate with."

Eugene grinned.

"Oh, Boris, you do know the way to my heart! Show me. Now, if not sooner."

"Right this way."

Hayes led Eugene further down the corridor, twisting and

turning, Eugene giddy with ecstasy, awaiting his delightful surprise.

And oh, what a delightful surprise it turned out to be.

Hayes reached the door, stood back, and with a widening smirk, he indicated the handle with a nod.

"After you."

Eugene practically danced to the door, opened it, then stood in amazement.

Before him, they stood.

His army.

But not that pathetic army that ran from a flamethrower. Not the pathetic army defeated by two people. Not the pathetic army that retreated at the first sign of hardship.

No, before him, in the grand hall, stood thousands of troops.

Every one of them injected with the synthesis they had successfully used on Donny.

Each one of them with the strength, speed, and capability to brush every other country aside.

Before him was the army Eugene had always intended to create.

And they were ready and raring to go.

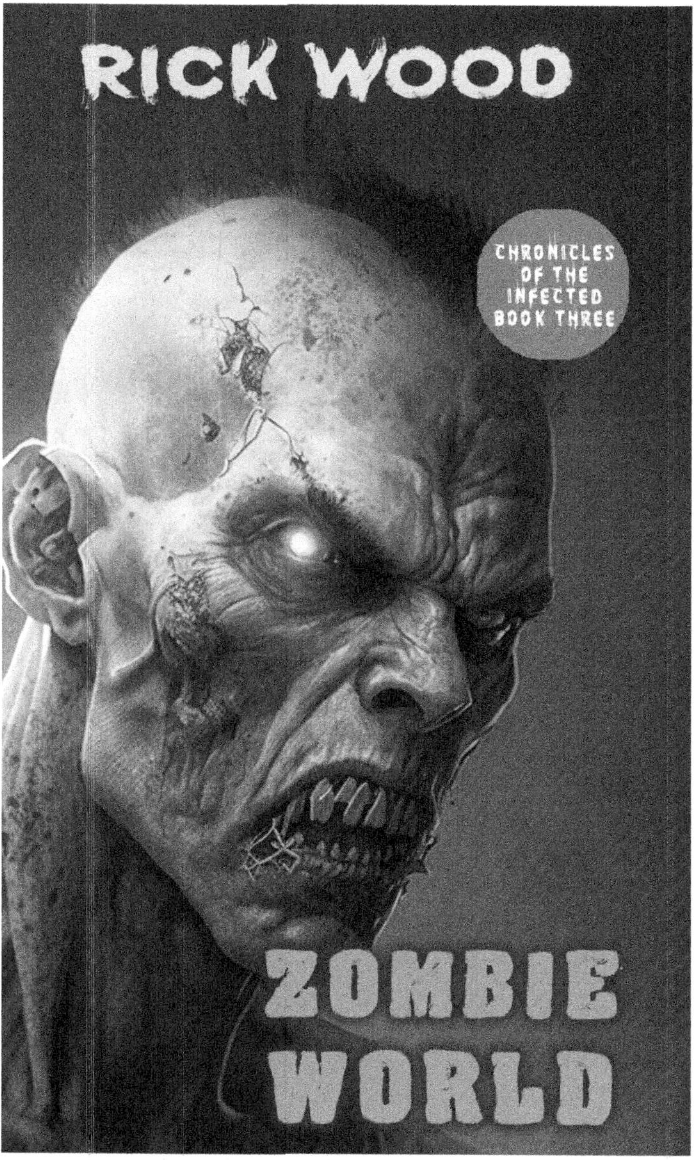
RICK WOOD
CHRONICLES OF THE INFECTED BOOK THREE
ZOMBIE WORLD

Would you like two free books?

Join Rick Wood's Reader's Group at www.rickwoodwriter.com/sign-up

BOOK ONE IN THE SENSITIVES SERIES
THE
SENSITIVES
RICK WOOD

RICK WOOD
CIA
ROSE
BOOK
ONE
WHEN THE
WORLD
HAS ENDED

BLOOD
SPLATTER
BOOKS
PSYCHO
B*TCHES
RICK WOOD
18+

About the Author

Rick Wood is a British writer born in Cheltenham.

His love for writing came at an early age, as did his battle with mental health. After defeating his demons, he grew up and became a stand-up comedian, then a drama and English teacher.

He now lives in Loughborough with his fiancée, where he divides his time between watching horror, reading horror, and writing horror.

Cover design by bloodsplatterpress.com

Copy-edited by LeeAnn @ FirstEditing.com

With thanks to my Street Team.

Printed in Great Britain
by Amazon

37317833R00158